by

J.A. Sommer

ILLUSTRATED BY
John D. Neiner

Bandersnatch Books

NORTH CAROLINA

This book is a work of fiction. References to real people, events, establishments, organizations, or locales are intended only to provide a sense of authenticity and are used to advance the fictional narrative. All other characters, and all incidents and dialogue, have galumphed from the author's imagination and are not to be construed as real.

Zao's Tales
Copyright © 2022 by J. A. Sommer

All rights reserved. No part of this book may be reproduced or transmitted in any form or by any means whatsoever without express written permission from the publisher, except in the case of brief quotations embodied in critical articles and reviews. Violators of this copyright may be subject to penalty or the wrath of fairy fire.

Printed in the United States of America
For information, address Bandersnatch Books.

P.O. Box 2473
Indian Trail, NC 28079
bandersnatchbooks.com
info@bandersnatchbooks.com
803.610.1223

Library of Congress Control Number: 2021947200
Hardcover ISBN: 978-0-9988454-8-7
Paperback ISBN: 978-0-9988454-9-4

DEDICATION

For my girls,
who helped start this particular dream.
May your life be filled with truth, beauty, righteousness,
and the greatest Person of all.

For my wife,
the first person who inspired me to tell a story.
"There is a truth inside of me... you were created for me."

CONTENTS

DEDICATION   *iii*
ACKNOWLEDGMENT   *vii*
PROLOGUE   *ix*
CHAPTER

1. The Book 1
2. The Feather and the Fairy 11
3. Searching for Meaning 25
4. The Library 35
5. Look to the Skies 49
6. Hold on Tight 61
7. The Lake 73
8. South Island 91
9. At Camp 113
10. Waking Up 123
11. Help 143
12. Captured 171
13. The Best Laid Plans... 187
14. Going Hunting 199
15. Preparations 221
16. It Begins 241
17. The Battle 263
18. The Battle Within 279
19. Questions and Answers 297
20. Home 315

ACKNOWLEDGMENT

A wise man once said, *"No man is an island, entire of itself."* For me, that means that what you see here is the collective labor of many people, each one somehow influencing the whole, though each person might not even know he or she had a part. I acknowledge the many patient reading teachers who taught this dyslexic to read, though it took many years. I am grateful to my parents who provided me with audio books to listen to, when that meant books on cassette tapes sent to our house from an initiative to help the blind, and who also read me the Greatest Book of all. I am so thankful for John Neiner, friend, kindred-spirit, and partner in crime. And last, but not least, the Bandies at Bandersnatch Books who helped get this book to the public.

—*J.A. Sommer*

PROLOGUE

A wise woman once said, "Read living books." Normal books are fine—those everyday stories found in the book-section of a superstore, the kinds of tales that a person reads to put themselves to sleep or pass the time on a rainy day—but those are not living books. Living books are just that: alive. In these books, Jacks kill giants, lions talk to the sons of Adam and daughters of Eve, and houses can fall on wicked witches. This tale is about just such a book.

A book that was so real, it was.

NAME	PRONUNCIATION	PAGE
Alsoomse	Al-**SOOM**-say	192
Andola	An-**DOLE**-ah	20
Aphina	A-**FEE**-na	3
Byrne	**BURN**	181
Frey	**FRAY**	7
Hetre	**HET**-er	140
Lili	**LIL**-ee	2
Manjula	Man-**JOOL**-ah	104
Nahtoosi	Na-**TOO**-see	193
Nizitapi	Nizz-i-**TOP**-ee	199
Perin	**PEAR**-in	136
Zao	**ZAY**-oh	29

CHAPTER 1

The Book

EFORE WE BEGIN, I MUST ADMIT THAT reading aloud was not the magic that unlocked this adventure, for that was a well-worn ritual in this little white house. Good books, reading aloud, and happy faces were a daily occurrence. After the fact, everyone involved agreed it must have been something about the book itself that brought about these strange events.

It was a Monday morning. Not the mid-winter kind where children are locked away in the classroom doing arithmetic, wishing to be playing in the snow, but the sunny summer kind—its happier cousin. The father of our story was away on a business trip, and his three daughters and wife were enjoying a present that he had sent them. The old saying goes, "Don't judge a book by its cover," and of all the books in the world this book proved it true. Its old leather binding was unassuming; a child would pass right by an old dusty tome like this in a library. But inside, the book's thick vellum pages were filled with hand-drawn sketches and pictures in the most brilliant colors. The flowing calligraphy even changed with the theme of each story. From the moment the cover was opened, it begged to be read. Some books simply demand a reader's attention.

Patty (the mother in our tale) sat in a sunny spot in the living room, a light breeze blowing through the screen door, and the girls gathered tightly around her listening. Their huddling was partly because of excitement and partly because of fear, the kind of fear caused by reading about villains that are very realistic. As she read, the moments passed unnoticed and the words enticed the children's imaginations. Carey, Ella, and Lili drank in every word. Patty knew her craft well. Years of practice had made reading aloud her specialty. She even changed accents and inflections as she switched from character to character. Entranced, the three blonde heads almost touched each other as they leaned in. Varying emotions flitted across their faces, mirroring sorrow, joy, or wonder depending on the mood of the passage. Though at this very moment, their faces were masks of excitement and fear.

"...*the sky filled with a black cloud, not of vapor or smoke, but of beating wings. Aphina had sent her minions, and it was time to perform her deadly commands,*" read Patty in a dramatic voice. Then Patty stopped reading. She had noticed her eight-year old daughter's brown eyes growing large and round. "Is the book too scary? We can stop reading for a while if you want me to."

Lili gave a determined shake of her head and replied, "No, no! Mama, please keep reading. I *do* want to hear what happens to the witch!"

The other heads bobbed in unison, and Carey, the oldest sister, put a protective arm around Lili's shoulders. Lili took a deep breath. "Can we *please* at least finish the chapter?"

Patty smiled. "Okay, where were we?" She settled back in and looked from the girls' eager faces to the leather volume propped in her lap. She began to read again. "*It was time to perform her deadly commands.*" Just then, the computer in the other room pulsed with the sounds of an incoming call and Patty stopped again.

"Daddy!" cried the girls, springing up from their seats. The book was abandoned on the coffee table. Four pairs of bare feet slapped the wood floor as they ran to the den. Patty tried to sit in her office chair in front of the computer but struggled as each girl fought for the best seats. They all wanted to perch on an armrest. After a few moments of bedlam (during which the chair was almost knocked over), everyone was finally sorted out. They were arranged precariously in front of the camera, but Patty was finally able to answer the call.

At that very moment something peculiar was happening in the next room. A sharp wind whistled through the screen door and turned a page in the old book. This first page turned slowly, but with ever-increasing speed, the wind caught and turned the pages. Then, just as suddenly as it began, it stopped. The tail end of the gust caught one last page, turning and flipping it gently. The room filled with an eerie calm as the wind rustled the curtain one last time before leaving. There, staring up from the newly turned page, was the painting of Aphina. Almost imperceptibly at first, the black ink used to paint her dress seemed to rise. It gathered and arced like a small soap bubble on the surface of a pan of water. Then, when it was no more than half the size of a bouncy ball, it burst, sending an inky mist into the air. The mist began to condense. It rolled and grew like a summer storm, boiling into a miniature, charcoal-black thundercloud. Within seconds the mist spread and formed an almost-six-foot-tall human figure. Then, she was simply there, beautiful Aphina, crow and all. She blinked with astonishment, her long-enameled fingernails reached to her shoulder, brushing back a wisp of blond hair, and stroked the feathers under her pet's chin. The habit had developed into a nervous kind of tick, something she did while thinking.

Her eyes darted around, taking in her strange surroundings, unlike any she had ever seen. "What trickery is this?" she whispered. She continued to search for understanding until her thoughts were shattered by a chorus of greetings in the next room.

"Daddy!" exclaimed happy young voices. Aphina was rooted to the ground. All she could do was listen. *Who are these people?*

"Hi, honey, how's your trip?" said a grown woman's voice.

"Great, beautiful," answered a male voice. "The project is coming along nicely. I've even had a little extra time for sight-seeing, though I wish you guys were here with me this time. Did you get the present?"

"Yep, got it in the mail this morning! We were just reading

it, in fact," the woman answered. "It's beautiful, John. You know, you really shouldn't have. You must've paid a fortune to have it shipped here so fast."

"Sure, I should have! Besides, my girls are worth it," the man replied. His tone was so affectionate that it turned Aphina's insides and caused her fingers to clench into fists.

"Daddy, Daddy, the book is great," interrupted the voice of a young girl. "The story we started with is sooo good. It's about these two girls, one's good and one's bad. Believe it or not, the princess named Aphina is the bad one. She's half elf. Her little sister and father die in this hunting accident—you know, the medieval kind with hounds and horses and blowing trumpets. And it was her fault—Aphina—I mean. She caused their deaths, or at least she thinks it was her fault. Well anyways, she gets angry because she thinks everyone blames her, and her stepmom won't talk to her. As she gets older, she gets more and more angry and then she decides to become a witch. Then when Aphina and Lendra grow up—that's the good one—they have to fight each other. At least I think so, we haven't got to that part yet. The story is so amazing!" By the end of her explanation, the girl was speaking so rapidly Aphina had difficulty understanding her. She was practically tripping over her words just to get the next one out.

"We were about to find out how Aphina was going to take over the surrounding kingdoms," added another girl. This was the voice of one burgeoning on adulthood while still holding the delicate softness and innocence of a child.

What was said next, Aphina could not have told. She was stunned to hear her life spoken of so plainly, the whole thing told as if it were a child's fairy story. Soon enough she was shaken from her deep reflections as she heard the father's voice speak again, "And what do you think of the story, Lili?"

Lily? That is my sister's name, thought the witch, as her chest tightened and tears formed in her eyes.

A happy voice answered him, the voice high pitched with excitement and filled with the magical tones of early childhood, "I can't wait to find out how the good guys defeat that wicked old witch in the end!"

Aphina staggered, grabbing her temples as if she had been slapped. Her sudden motion caused her crow to hop awkwardly on her right shoulder, but it managed to keep its balance. *Old?* the princess thought indignantly. *Why, who do these insolent people think they are? I will show them no one can mock the High Queen of Frey.* She looked about the room for her magical staff and noticed the book for the first time. There, staring up from the page was an exact painting of her likeness, as if someone had stolen a portrait from the royal gallery and reproduced it in this book. Mystified, she watched as the picture on the page faded away. *What dark magic is this? Could it be true? Have I been trapped inside those pages by some powerful wizard?* Her temples continued to throb as she picked up the volume to scan its pages.

Even now in the midst of her anger, she allowed herself a fleeting moment to cradle the book in her arms so that she might admire its quality. Skimming the pages, she moved away from the voices in the other room but froze half-way to the open door. There it was, written in black ink, spelled out plainly: her defeat. Her revenge, all her long-laid plans—destroyed. *But how,* she thought, *how could this be true? Could this magic book have me locked away? Does it control my destiny somehow?* Then she saw those fateful words that end so many fairy stories, *"...they lived happily ever after."* Her mind screamed, *Not if I can help it!* Quicker than a flash, before she could feel guilty for harming this work of art, she snatched a long, curved dagger from her belt. With a skilled hand she cut out the last pages from her story and placed the leaves into her leather satchel. She was sheathing her knife when a creaking sound from the next room drew her from her brooding thoughts. Instinct from years of training and scheming set in. Her spider-like mind began spinning webs. *I need to hide*, she thought. *Watch from the shadows; take account of my assets; plan. That is the only way to win this war,* Aphina decided. *Soon I will gather enough strength to get my revenge. Then, oh, then, I will make these strange people regret the day they thought of mocking my life with their magical little book.*

While the strangers in the other room were saying their goodbyes, the black clad figure placed the book back on the table. Deftly she clutched her pet's beak shut and plucked out one of its feathers. Then she removed a glass vial from her satchel and dusted the feather with small white shining granules, which looked something like sparkling salt. She set the feather down beside the book then passed through the screen door and escaped as silently as a fleeing shadow. The only signs of her visit were the pages she had removed and a single black crow's feather.

CHAPTER 2

The Feather and the Fairy

A WARNING TICKLED AT THE BACK OF Patty's mind as she entered the living room. *Something's wrong,* she thought. The feeling was similar to the moment right before you realize that your school notebook has been left at home...the one with your completed homework in it.

The girls settled back into the couch, like a family of little birds wiggling back into their nest. Sitting in her armchair, Patty reached for the book. That was when she noticed that some of the pages had been cut.

"What in the world?" she said. She inspected the damaged pages. *What had someone done to this beautiful book? How could they?*

"What, Mom?" asked Carey, as all three girls scrambled off the couch. They came to inspect what their mother was staring at.

"The book! That's so strange. I don't remember any damage when I flipped through it. I mean, the whole end of the story is missing," Patty explained. The girls leaned over the coffee table to get a closer look.

"Mom, what's this?" Ella said, tilting her strawberry-blonde head to the side. Her eyebrows crinkled as she held up a long black feather between her fingers. "Where'd this come from?"

"Where did you get that?" asked Lili, who was tired of staring at the injured book.

"Let me see that," said Patty, carefully taking the feather from her daughter's outstretched hand. "That's odd. It looks like a crow's feather...kinda like the ones that we used for nature studies last month, but I could have sworn that I got rid of all of them."

"It sure does look like one, Mom," said Ella, "though I don't remember them being so big. And I know they weren't this shiny!"

Everyone sat back down, a bit perplexed. Patty and the youngest two children continued to inspect the feather. Though the others were interested in the feather, Carey decided she would rather investigate their damaged storybook.

Mindlessly she began flipping through the pages distracting herself with the book's artwork. "Mom, didn't this book have a picture of Aphina in it? You know, the full page one, the one you showed us?"

Doggedly now, Carey turned the pages in chunks and then flipped back page by page as she sought in vain for the illustration. Finally, she stopped at page fifty-eight. It was blank. At its bottom in small italic letters was written the name 'Aphina.'

"That's so strange," Carey whispered to herself. Unable to find what she was looking for, she contented herself by turning back to an illustration she could find. Her frustration boiled over as she murmured to herself, "Who cuts up a beautiful book anyways?"

Ella heard her sister's mumbled question. "Maybe that's why someone sold it. Dad got a good deal because it was a damaged book!" She had just returned from a quick sprint to the study, where she had retrieved a magnifying glass so they could get a closer look at the feather. Patty and Ella continued to inspect the sparkling specimen while Lili dug around in the tower of schoolbooks stacked near the sofa. She was looking for her nature journal. As a matter of habit, she knew she should try and sketch this one-of-a-kind find.

Gazing at the open pages before her, Carey began rereading one of the passages that had thrilled her that morning. She hoped to relive the images in her mind and experience again the emotions they evoked. The paragraphs she was reading sat opposite an artist's rendition that captured the scene perfectly. The sketch depicted the poor young heroine, Lendra, walking through the crowds and stopping to talk with a fairy seller at a night carnival.

The words rolled unconsciously from Carey's lips as she began to read aloud.

"Above the seller, who had intentionally donned bright and colorful mismatched clothes for the festival, were the fairies. Each lantern encased a single fairy in a paper prison. The round lanterns looked like tiny moons floating in the night sky. Each was suspended by a thin flaxen string tied to a long straight rod. The lanterns, constructed of thin parchment stretched over balsam wood frames, were illumined with the glimmering light of fairy fire. At that moment each one burned with a hue of a different color, one blue, one red, one green, and one yellow. Lendra stared in wonder, watching

the lanterns flicker with a rhythmic pulse as the wings of the fairies fluttered inside their enclosures like butterflies..."

Suddenly everyone else stopped looking at the crow's feather. Carey's reading aloud filled the air with magic. All the hairs on their arms were standing on end, as if they were charged with static electricity. The words had taken on a life of their own. Everyone could almost hear the pennants slapping in the wind. They were engulfed with the cheerful buzz of the crowds. They were enticed by the cries of the hawkers. Somehow, it was as if the gap between the happy land of childhood imagination and the predictable world of reality had been bridged.

The scene enveloped Carey and she was forced to stop reading. As her last words faded away, a burning spark suddenly jumped out of the page. It shot from the illustration like an ember popping out of a campfire. As it burned and tumbled along the coffee table, it was followed by more and more sparks. Each one popped and crackled as it shot out from the surface of the page. It seemed as if someone had hidden a Roman candle in the book. As the number of sparks increased, they fanned out in a circle as large as the entire table. Then the tiny glowing sparks drew together, like metal shavings being drawn to a powerful magnet. As they gathered closer and closer, they rose from the table. Rising, they danced like a swarm of fireflies on a warm summer's night. They merged to form a single pulsing orb, and a sudden gust of wind filled the room. It carried with it the smell of bonfires, the sound of children's laughter, and the sugary scent of candied fruits.

All sat there in stunned silence, their mouths hanging open in amazement. Four pairs of eyes, three blue and one brown, watched and grew wider with each passing moment. The scrap pieces of paper on the nearby end tables rustled and fluttered as this giggling ball of pulsing light rippled.

Everyone leaned in for a closer look while Carey moved to poke at it with her index finger. They flinched as the light flared up with such intensity that they saw spots floating before their eyes. As the light dimmed, delicate little wings began to unfurl from it. They looked like frost growing on a cold windowpane. Next came two arms and two legs. They stretched out like the petals of a flower waking to the sun. When the light finally dimmed to a gentle glow, there before their eyes was a little fairy dressed in an outfit made from the petals of a snowdrop. Her pretty little head was crowned with short curly blonde hair. She was delicate and beautiful. Ella and Lili could hardly believe how tiny she was, as she stood there on top of their open book.

The little figure slowly flapped her wings as she inspected

them for any signs of damage. She straightened the petals of her dress fastidiously. Totally oblivious to her surroundings, the delicate, almost child-like face grinned, and she spoke to herself in a tiny voice. "Well, not too much worse for the wear. Ohh, how I hate those paper lanterns!" she protested in frustration.

Just as the fairy turned to face the onlookers, the awe and astonishment of the moment was punctured by Lili as she airily breathed out, "It's a fairy!"

With these words everyone seemed to regain their senses and the fairy at last noticed her surroundings. The next instant the younger two girls were moving in with cupped hands, as if they were going to catch a grasshopper, while Carey continued to sit there with her mouth hanging wide open.

"It must be magic!" exclaimed Ella.

"This is amazing," Carey gasped.

Their mother raised her index finger to her lips and quietly shushed them. She had noticed how shocked the fairy was and did not want her to fly away. Patty motioned the girls to back up very slowly while she herself moved in more closely. She held her palm open, hoping the fairy would land, but just like a bird flies away when you try to get too close, the fairy darted off, leaving a trail of fiery sparks right up to the corner of the ceiling.

"Aww," complained Lili. "It's okay. We won't hurt you!"

Hearing this kind remark the fairy smiled and seemed to consider coming back.

"Don't worry. We don't have any lanterns anyway," added Ella, trying to help, though with that little reminder of captivity the fairy frowned and shrank back into the corner.

"Way to help, Ella." Carey rolled her eyes.

"Well, at least I am trying to do somethin' instead of sitting around with my mouth hanging open," retorted Ella.

Hearing the bickering, the fairy's fire changed from a bright fearful blue to a deeply annoyed purple, her mood changing to match the frustrated words.

"Girls, please! You're not helping," Patty scolded. After a few moments of calm, she spoke more softly to the fairy. "Hello there, my name is Patty. These are my daughters, Carey, Ella, and Lili." As she spoke, she pointed to each girl in turn. "What's your name?"

Hearing these kind words and noticing their friendly tone, the fairy's glow changed to a happy yellow. Standing to her full height and lifting one leg as if she were skating on a frozen pond, the fairy glided about five feet closer to the floor, though she made sure that she was still well out of reach. "I don't think you could say my fairy name. Most people can't," the fairy replied with her nose turned up in air, then added, "but my human name is Mackay."

"It's nice to meet you, Mackay," replied all the girls politely.

Mackay gave a mocking little bow, then dove as if jumping into a lake and sped toward Patty. When she reached eye-level she pulled up dramatically and sat down cross-legged in midair. Simpering, she smiled, very pleased with all of the attention. Waves of yellow fairy fire rippled from her as she fluttered her wings.

"So, what kind of magic did you all use to get me here? There I was in the middle of the Full Moon Festival trying not to attract the attention of any of the boys from the castle. Those are the ones that like to buy fairies just to pull their wings off. They're beastly!" this last part she added with a shudder. Thinking of having her wings pulled off had given her a painful pinched expression. "Anyway, next thing I know, I'm here... where is here anyway?" The fairy's words had a way of running into each other when she was excited, adding to the musical quality of her voice. Her accent was lilting, like a soft breeze. It swept one along, so much so that it seemed very hard to correct her impudence.

"You're in Center Lake," answered Lili politely.

"The lake district? That far? But how did I end up in Andola?" asked Mackay.

"Andola? Uh...no, Center Lake, Michigan!" corrected Ella.

"Mit...chi...gun! Never heard of it. You all are very strange aren't you, but what should I expect? Look at your clothes and house. You must have funny ways in Mitch-i-gun!" Mackay said, shaking her head. She looked them over disapprovingly but seemed quite curious about their house.

Everyone sat back down as Patty posed the next question.

"Mackay. You do understand that you're not in Andola? You're not even in the Kingdom of the Eight Crowns anymore. You're in the real world. I mean, you came out of that book." Patty explained this slowly as she pointed at the storybook for emphasis. "Do you know how you did it?"

"This is all rather curious. How should I know? You're the witches," said Mackay as she flew down to get a closer look at the book. "All I know is that I am free from my lantern. As long as no fairy catchers get me, or Aphina doesn't feed me to one of her hawks for lunch, I am more than content," Mackay explained. When she mentioned Aphina's name her whole body shivered as if blasted by a winter's wind.

"Wait," Patty said abruptly. "Carey, turn back to that empty page again."

For a moment the only sounds that could be heard were the flittering of tiny wings and the turning of vellum pages. Carey's fingertip tapped on the empty page. "Here you go, Mom," Carey said, as she handed over the book. "But I don't see what's so important about it."

As Patty placed the book on her lap, Ella peered at the page. Before her mother could say a word, she blurted out, "Look Mom. It says Aphina at the bottom. It's like some kind of caption. You don't think..." Ella trailed off.

"I do, but I am hoping I'm wrong," said Patty. "I want to check one more thing to make sure," she explained as she searched the book. Very quickly she found the page with the festival painted on it.

"Look, girls," Patty pointed, "look at the middle lantern. It's dim, and there's no light coming from it. The fairy inside is gone." As Patty's words sank in, their heads turned and four sets of eyes stared at the fairy who happened to be dancing in circles while giving them all an impish smile.

Patty slowly took the crow's feather from Ella's trembling hand and showed it to Mackay.

"Mackay, have you ever seen Aphina and her crow before?" She paused and took a breath. She was trying to think of the best way to frame her question. "I mean, would you be able to identify a feather from one of Aphina's crows?"

"Of course! I saw her and some of her fairy killers at a castle feast once," Mackey replied defensively, "but I'd rather not talk about it. Besides, it doesn't matter anyway. If we're in Mitch-a-gun like you said, she's far away. And I say good riddance!" Mackay punctuated that last part by spitting. Trying to distract herself, she flew over to the black feather in Patty's hand. It was several inches longer than her whole body. As she reached out to inspect it, the shining dust that covered it caught her eye.

"Smelly trolls and poisonous mushrooms, I think that's Night Shade Dust and maybe something else! Where *did* you get that? That's *bad* medicine, only witches and warlocks use that..." Mackay stopped short. She looked at the feather again. Then, as she reconsidered the girls and grown woman sitting beside her she began to shy away. Her fairy fire turned to an uncertain blueish gray.

"Mackay," Patty began urgently. She used her hand to gently corral the fairy and bring her closer to her face as she bent over. "Nightshade Dust... is that the kind of magic that a witch like Aphina would use?"

"Sure, she uses it on all her winged henchmen. It deforms them. They become bigger than nature intended and then they have to obey all of her commands. It also makes them very irritable. Why?" Mackay said.

The girls looked puzzled, but for Patty the pieces had snapped into place. The cut book. The black feather. The fairy. Patty sat quietly for a moment. She let the girls think it over for themselves. She waited and watched each girl's eyes as they slowly put the facts together.

The full implication of these words settled on Lili, and the little girl leaned closer to her mother. Then she asked, "Mom, is it true? Is Aphina really alive?"

"I'm afraid so Lili-lou. I'm not sure how, but we've got to find a way to get her back into this book."

CHAPTER 3

Searching for Meaning

HOW DOES A PERSON FEEL WHEN DOING something that has never been done before? What were the thoughts of Zorro, that apprentice of Leonardo Da Vinci, as he tested the first flying machine? Did he feel panic right before he flapped, paddled, and prayed? Are there words to describe the feelings one experiences when the locked door to the imaginary suddenly pops open and the impossible somehow becomes completely possible? Maybe it is like the feeling a person gets right between the eyes, the biting cold and painful numbness caused by eating ice cream too quickly.

This was the frost that settled on everyone's minds, and they all sat there staring at one another. But just as quickly as the numbness came, it passed, and as it faded away each person took a deep breath. There was nothing else to do but ready themselves for the task ahead. *What should we do now?* they all wondered, though no one spoke it aloud.

Finally, Carey stirred herself and said what everyone else was thinking: "What are we going to do, Mom?" Her worry was evident in the tone of her voice.

"Well," Patty answered after a brief pause. The look in her blue eyes and the set of her jaw was a mask of determination. She *would* take the necessary steps forward, no matter how she felt. Slapping her knees with the palms of her open hands, she pushed up from the couch. Then she walked over and grabbed a pen and paper from the items scattered on the table. "You know what your Dad would say," she added before she sat back down. "'When you don't know what to do, start by asking yourself some questions.'" As she sat, she punctuated her last words with a click of her pen, "So, let's do it."

"Let's do what?" asked Lili, who had missed her mother's point.

"We need to ask some questions, but they can't be just any questions. The key to this whole thing will be to ask the right questions!" Patty explained, trying to sound positive. Prepared for inspiration, she held the pad of yellow ruled paper and sat poised to record their thoughts.

"What do we know?" she asked.

"We're in big trouble!" answered Carey dramatically.

"No. What do we know that will help us, Carey? Come on, let's think!" Patty knew the only way they were going to get somewhere was to change gears. They needed to clear their minds of all the gloom and doom that surrounded them.

"Well, it looks like a witch just popped out of our reading book!" offered Ella, scrunching her face and biting her lip.

"Okay…a witch has come out of our book," mumbled Patty as she scribbled the words on the note pad. "Anyone have any ideas what she might be doing?"

"You mean, besides trying to take over the world and kill us?" replied Carey.

"Haha, very funny," said Patty flatly, then added with a raised eyebrow, "I meant, we have to try and think like her. Get inside her head. We need to try and remember all we can about her. Maybe the best thing we can do would be to look at the book again. That seems like a good place to start."

Carey shrugged her shoulders, then picked up the book and thumbed through the remaining pages, as Ella peered over her shoulder. "There's not much left," said Carey. "It looks like

Aphina must've cut out most of the pages to her story. So, we'll have to go by memory. Though after all this craziness, my brain feels a little scrambled."

"A *little* scrambled?" Ella asked. Carey's response was to cross her eyes and stick out her tongue good naturedly. Ella smiled with one of her devilish grins then turned her attention back to the book. But after thinking it over for a few moments, her mood changed.

"Uh, Mom, how're we gonna have an idea what she would do? We haven't even finished her story, and I for one can't seem to remember anything. There's been a little too much excitement. Maybe it would be different if we had the whole story or something..." Ella said.

"Why not get a new copy of the book?" asked Lili.

Patty's eyes shot up from her writing pad, and she looked into Lili's innocent brown eyes. "Lili-lou, that is a great idea!" Patty said as she bent over and kissed the little forehead.

"Girls, grab that book and follow me," commanded Patty as she jumped up from the couch and went into the den.

Once Patty entered the next room, she sat right down in her old wooden office chair. It looked like something out of a black-and-white private detective movie, the shows their grandfather loved to watch. That was why the girls liked it so much. As their mom always said—it had character. After setting down her pad of paper and pen she tapped the spacebar on the keyboard to wake up the screen. "Here we go," she said. The girls pulled in three chairs from around the dining table, and Mackay hovered above Patty's shoulder. She was curious and quiet, watching all the activity.

"What's the book's name again?" asked Patty.

Carey, adopting a proper British accent, read, "*An Anthology of Fairy Tales from Around the World.*"

Patty's fingers tapped away on the keyboard as she repeated the title out loud to herself. One second the words filled the search bar, the next the screen read "No results found. Try without quotes." The page was filled with related searches, but after scanning through the first few links, Patty knew she would have to try something else.

"Well, okay, let's try the author's name," Patty said as she typed 'Zao Cadmus' into the search bar. Enter. The screen pulsed to life and the search results filled the screen.

"There we go. Wikipedia. That should help." Patty clicked the first link. The page popped open. The article was titled in bold black text with the author's name. On the right side sat a black and white picture of a distinguished looking gentlemen with robust Greek features, thick wavy salt and pepper hair, and a short, trim black beard. After scrolling down the page and then back to the top again, Patty started reading the first paragraph aloud.

"Zao Cadmus, (29 November 1898 – 22 November 1963) was a professor, author, artist, and literary historian. The third of eleven children, Zao was born into an immensely wealthy and ancient Greek family. After completing his basic education in Greece, Zao traveled to England to further his studies. He was accepted into Oxford University where he completed multiple degrees. Five years after graduation he was taken on as a professor of ancient literature and philosophy at Oxford University (1930 – 1963 Magdalen College). While teaching, he did extensive research on international mythology, ethnic fairy tales, and folk lore... blah, blah, blah. Okay, this might help us." Patty added, starting to paraphrase, "He had a very private life. He never married and spent the last fifteen years of his life devoting himself entirely to the mastery of book binding, calligraphy, and illustration, outside of his time as a lecturer. He died at the age of 64 after a short battle with pneumonia."

"Great! Now what? If he's dead, what're we going to do? We're definitely not going to ask him any questions," Ella huffed.

"We can't talk to the author, but maybe we can buy another

copy. Let's try over at Amazon, Mom. Maybe they'll have a digital copy," suggested Carey.

"Well, you never know what we'll find," replied Patty while opening Amazon's website in another tab. "Zao Cadmus." Patty said the name as she typed it and sent off her search. Once the results popped on screen she added, "Gotcha!" They all leaned in to inspect the list on the screen, "All right, what do we have here? No digital copies, but there are a few Greek copies of the book. That won't help. And it looks like one used English copy. Bingo! Here we go. Buy from a seller. Okay... and the seller is... from Hungary. Three hundred fifty dollars! Expect thirty days before deliver... what? Where's that guy live? Some kind of monastery or something?" Patty grumbled. She rubbed her temples then exhaled. Releasing the tension in her neck and shoulders, she tried to calm herself. As she looked away from the screen, Patty noticed Lili. Her little face was staring intently at the computer, and the glowing white light was shining in her concerned eyes. Patty patted her head to reassure her and received a smile with the front two teeth missing in return. "Well," she said, "let's see if someone else has a copy."

They searched on Barnes and Noble, Books-a-Million, Alibris, Ebay, Folio Society, every last major online bookstore they could think of and then multiple independent bookstores that had searchable websites. After thirty minutes of looking, they had to admit there was nothing. It was either unavailable or would take weeks to ship, not to mention it was also incredibly expensive.

"Now what?" asked Ella.

"I just go to the library when I want a book, Mama. How about that?" asked Lili. "We could try that old castle-like library downtown; it's got lots of big old books!"

"Well, it's worth a shot. The children's librarian has been there forever, and she does have an amazing collection. Fact is, we're not getting anywhere on the internet," Patty said standing up. "No wonder I am a Luddite at heart," she added under her breath.

Patty entered the living room again. After crossing the room, she grabbed her keys from a little Bolga basket on the console table by the front door. "You guys grab your shoes and you grab the book, okay Carey?" Patty looked at Mackay. "Now what are we going to do with you?" Mackay was looking at herself in the mirror that was resting on the table. The fairy shifted back and forth between making funny faces in the glass and admiring her petite figure. "We definitely can't leave you here, that's for sure," Patty said to herself as Mackay started exploring the tabletop. She knocked around the little clay bowls, smelled the scented candles, and almost broke a one-of-a-kind decorative plate John had bought during one of his more recent trips.

"Mackay," Patty said, trying to sound cheerful and not frustrated, "do you think that you could come on a trip with us? You know we're probably going to need your help once we get a copy of the book."

"Sure," Mackay said. Her fairy fire had turned into a very

proud orange. "I can come along. It might be nice to see a castle library, even if it is in Mitch-i-gun!"

"Great!" Patty said.

The older girls came back with their shoes on. Lili was the last to arrive. She was scooting along, stopping every other step as she tried to get her right shoe on. All the way from the steps she had been walking half-bent over, digging at her heel with her finger. The back of the shoe had crumpled in her haste, so she was having trouble getting it on right. She finally got her foot in all the way as she reached the front door. There she stood trying to look straight and tall, like a soldier, though both shoelaces were untied.

"Carey, you got the book, right?" Patty asked. Carey answered with a nod. "Ella, you make sure Mackay makes it to the car," Patty said. The fairy had started pulling stamps off the roll in one of the bowls and was sticking them to the wall. "And Lili," Patty added as she knelt to help her tie her laces, "are you all ready for this kiddo?" Once she had finished the last bow, she knelt there looking into the seven-year-old's big eyes.

"Sure, Mom," answered Lili with a grin, "let's go find that book. I wanna find out what happens to that witch!" Patty kissed the brave little head before standing up. Taking her daughter's hand, they headed out the front door to the car.

CHAPTER 4

The Library

"THAT'S A VERY STRANGE CARRIAGE YOU have there," laughed Mackay, twinkling with yellow light. They had walked down the short sidewalk that led to the driveway and opened the doors to the family's green vintage Volkswagen Beetle. As they did, Mackay made another comment. "It looks like a metal frog!"

"It's a car, Mackay," explained Ella. "Besides, it's cute!"

Soon they were flying down the country roads. The wind was blowing in their hair and everything seemed a little more normal as they looked out at the small farms and orchards with their roadside stands. The rolling hills were covered with a patchwork of old farms and modern homes. Each patch was stitched to the main road by a long gravel driveway. Mackay found out the hard way that she could not hover with the windows open, not with all that wind blowing through the car. After smacking her head against the roof a few times, it was not too difficult to convince her to perch on Ella's shoulder. From there she could easily watch out the window. After about ten minutes of driving they rounded a bend and came to the outskirts of town.

    The girls loved their little town. It was not like a typical old town with one main road, a grocery store, and a tiny public school. No, Center Lake had once dreamed of being a city, though that had been seventy years ago when the town and manufacturing were growing. Back then there were new factories and jobs being created. That was when 'downtown' had been built. During the 'boom', five whole blocks had been expectantly constructed. Not long after, most of them were filled with tall, serious, stony-faced buildings. The truth is, many things about the town had changed over the years, but despite the changes, the girls still liked downtown the best. Though most of its citizens did not go there on a daily basis anymore, the kids loved going there whenever they had the chance. The copper-domed city hall, the courthouse, the castle library, and the Temple Theater were among the old buildings that still had regular business. They were the last holdovers from the 'good old days.' The girls thought they were interesting enough to look at, but what made downtown really great was all the new exciting things tucked into the bottom floors of all those other old buildings. Carey always thought it looked like the buildings were wearing stylish tennis shoes underneath their formal ball gowns. The new park and playground with its giant spraying fountain that they liked to run through on hot days, the children's science museum they visited at least once a year, and the tourist traps and restaurants that everyone came to enjoy while visiting the many surrounding lakes gave all those stodgy gray stones splashes of vibrant color. Besides, the little fudge shops, ice cream parlors, candle makers, and saltwater taffy pullers attracted summer business and filled the air with both salty and sweet aromas that made the girls' mouths water.

As Patty turned onto Main Street, she was relieved to find that everything seemed relatively quiet this week. Last week had been the vintage car show and downtown had been packed with thousands of visitors and every kind of hot rod imaginable. When she reached Fifth Street she hit her blinker and turned onto the last main road. In a few moments she was entering the parking lot opposite the newspaper building. It sat across from the library and kitty-corner to the Center Lake Chronicle building. She had no problem finding a parking spot, as the Chronicle had its own private lot and story time at the library was not until tomorrow.

"Lili and Carey, you guys can come on in with me, but Ella, you had better stay in the car with Mackay. I don't think taking a fairy into the library is a good idea," said Patty, shutting off the engine.

"No-o-o, I'm not staying here! This place is unbelievable! I've never been in a castle library like that, and besides, you said I could be helpful!" Mackay stated her case quite matter-of-factly as she crossed her arms with a stubborn scowl. Her fairy fire flashed so intensely it formed a bright red halo around her little blonde head.

"Mackay, you're not in the book anymore, remember?" Her voice was high- pitched and syrupy, like when she was trying to coax Lili into some kind of decision. "People *here* haven't seen fairies before and when they do, they might have lots of questions," Carey explained.

"Nonsense! I'm not staying," protested Mackay. Without another word, she flew out the car's open window and perched on top of a nearby lamp post. The ornate ten-foot-tall post had been decorated with a pennant emblazoned with the town's name, and Mackay in all her defiant glory looked down on them like a little queen perched on top of an impenetrable stone tower.

"Mackay! You come back here right now," called Ella with an exasperated cry as she got out of the car. She marched over to the lamp post, scanning the parking lot for onlookers. *The last thing we need is for someone to see her,* Ella thought. Fortunately, no one was around just then. That, of course, was due to the fact that it was a warm summer's day, which means one of two things in Michigan: everybody was either at the lake, or inside sitting in front of their air conditioners.

Just as Ella reached the lamp post, she got an idea. "What if I read you a story?" suggested Ella as she looked up at the angry little fairy.

Mackay peered down from her perch. Ella's question had piqued her interest. "What *kind* of story?" she asked.

"One of the ones from the book," answered Ella. "How's that sound?"

"Fine, but it had better be a good one," Mackay pouted. She came down from the lamp post ever so slowly, pretending she was an elegant princess walking down a long spiral staircase, her tiny hand resting on a banister which did not really exist. When Mackay finally reached her, Ella hustled her back to the car. Within moments, she was seated back in the car and the fairy was hovering above her shoulder. The little figure was so fully engaged and distracted by the prospect of a story, she was bathed in a contented yellow glow, all her protests forgotten for the present.

With that little problem taken care of, Patty could focus on the matter at hand. She turned to her second born and gave her a knowing look, then added an order with raised eyebrows, "Ella, no stories with bad guys. Got it?" Patty sighed and took a second to collect her thoughts, then addressed her other daughters. "Now that that's settled, we'll go inside and see what we can find. Ella, you and Mackay will have to climb in the back. That should keep you guys from being noticed. You can pop the windows open back there, but I think I'll have to put the front windows up, at least part of the way. That way, if anyone passes by on the sidewalk they'll think we don't want the car getting too hot." When the windows were partially rolled up she removed the key from the ignition and put it in her purse. After some intense rummaging she pulled out her library card. Brandishing it in the air, she said, "Let's go girls. Be back as fast as we can. And Ella? Stay out of sight."

After Ella climbed into her assigned spot she slouched in the back seat. She sat so low she felt like she was sitting on the floor and she was sure she was going to have a horrible crick in her neck. All she could hope was that the local sheriff would not drive by. If he spied her alone in a parked car he would surely come to ask where her mother was and that would start who knows how many more problems. She shuddered at the thought of it. *No sir, my mother is not here, she's in the library. Yes sir, that is in fact a fairy!* Looking over at Mackay, Ella considered her options and hoped for her mother to hurry back. *What story can I read you that won't cause too much trouble?* she thought.

Just then she noticed that the little figure was sitting up straight and tall (well, as tall as a person that size can), leaning against the back of the seat. Every bit of her restrained composure resembled a toddler forcing herself to sit still, because her teacher had promised her a piece of candy for being extra quiet. Though Mackay was suppressing her endless energy as best she knew how, it still came bubbling to the surface like fizz in a glass of soda pop. All about her was a faint yellow aura and, try as she might, she could not keep from tapping the toes of her green slippers together. Her little hazel eyes were filled with sparkles. Ella knew that Mackay's patience would only last so long, so she flipped through the storybook purposefully. At the halfway point an illustration caught her eye. The story that accompanied the picture was only five pages long and had only the one drawing. It was quite whimsical and depicted little gnomes working in a garden. The funny little men with long white beards and red or green hats seemed harmless enough. *No bad guys,* thought Ella, checking off her mother's instruction from her mental list. *Well, let's give it a try.*

"*Once upon a time, there was a little glade next to a bubbling spring,*" began Ella as Mackay slid closer. The points of the fairy's little ears rose and seemed to stand on end like a bunny rabbit's. There would be no problems keeping her out of trouble at this point.

Five minutes passed and Ella was satisfied that nothing *really* unusual had happened... well, except for the five two-inch tall gnomes that were crawling all over the back seat. In the midst of her reading they had simply popped out of the book like mushrooms.

Each one wore a red cone-shaped hat and a bright blue coat encircled with a wide leather belt which restrained a chubby belly. Their white beards cascaded down to their knees like foaming waterfalls, and each gnome wore a pair of wooden clogs painted in different bright colors. Then Ella noticed their tiny little tools: rakes, hoes, and shovels. She sure hoped they wouldn't ruin the car's seats. It was a vintage rebuild, after all. Fortunately for her, she had only a paragraph left to go before she finished the story. Her only concern was whether her mom would get back before the gnomes got into any real trouble. Thus far the worst thing they had done was to leave muddy little footprints all over the clean white leather seats.

By now she was too distracted to really enjoy the story. Duty-bound to finish after giving her word to Mackay, Ella droned on and on in an endless chant of meaningless words. She did not feel like reading. Just before she read the last line, she stopped to wipe her forehead with the back of her hand. It *was* hot, but she was certain most of her sweat was caused by all the anxiety stoking her nerves. Ella took a deep breath and with determination blurted out the ending of the story, "*...and the gnomes saved the Ever-Blossom and lived happily ever after. The end.*" Her voice held a joyful finality as she read the last two words. Silence followed, and it was punctuated by a contented sigh from Mackay.

"That was a good story! May we read another one?" asked Mackay.

Just as Ella opened her mouth to give an answer to Mackay, the gnomes perked up their ears. It was as if they heard someone calling their names. They joyously danced a little jig, each one skipping and jumping up onto the open book while waving their little hands goodbye, then they slowly faded away. Each gnome dissolved into a sparkling tendril of mist which snaked through the warm summer air and seeped into the book like water drawn into a dry sponge.

Mackay jumped, her eyes wide. "There you go doing your ju-ju again," she said. She was hovering where the gnomes had been just moments before and her fairy fire was winking in and out, switching between shades of yellow and blue. Struck dumb with disbelief, she waved her hand through the air where the gnomes had been. Maybe they had only been made invisible.

"Could it be that simple?" Ella asked to no one in particular as she closed the book. "We just have to finish the...?"

Ella did not get to finish her thought, though. Her mind was jerked to a stop when the driver's door popped open. She jumped out of her skin and gasped, clutching at her chest. Her pulse thrummed in her ears and she tried to calm her breathing, as her mother pulled the seat forward to allow Lili to get inside.

"You guys sure know how to startle somebody," Ella said. Lili crawled into the back seat with a happy little grin on her face. Pulling the front seat back into place a little too excitedly she turned to see how *her* little fairy was doing.

Patting Mackay on the head with the tip of her finger, Lili asked Ella, "Was Mackay good?"

"Of course! We fairy folk are always on our best behavior," answered Mackay with a naughty grin.

"Did you get the book?" asked Ella once she climbed out and let Carey get in the back. (She had won the best two out of three in rock, paper, scissors, after all, and was not going to lose out on riding up front).

"Nope, the librarian said she'd never heard of it," answered Patty, then quoted in a high-pitched and wobbly voice just like the librarian's, "I have been working here for the last forty-five years, and I know *all* the good books, dearie." With a chuckle she added, "She did finally check the computer for us after some kind prodding. How did it go out here?" asked Patty.

"Fine. Well, besides the five gnomes that came out of the book."

"Gnomes? Really? That's cool!" interrupted Lili. She

searched around for the little creatures like a child hunting for the last hidden Easter egg, then added, "but where are they?"

"They're gone," Ella answered.

"*Please* tell me they didn't get away. The last thing we need today is to be chasing garden gnomes all over downtown," said Patty. At that moment she looked very tired as she sat there staring blankly out the front window while massaging her forehead with her fingertips.

"No, they just disappeared. Just like Mackay, they came out of the picture when I was reading and spent the rest of the story trying to hoe the car seats, but the moment I finished their story they waved good-bye and disappeared."

"It was some serious ju-ju," mumbled Mackay, her body flickering light blue while she sat cross-legged on top of the door lock like it was some kind of giant stool. She had flittered over to her perch hoping to see something interesting, but now sat hunched over with a look of utter boredom on her little pouting face.

"I think that's how it works, Mom. When we finish their story, the characters go back into the book," said Ella.

"Then that's the answer! We just have to get the story back, read it, and Aphina will disappear," said Carey wide-eyed.

"I don't know that it's all that simple, but at least it's a beginning," interjected Patty as she fished in her bag for her keys. "Buckle up. The sooner we get home, the sooner we can come up with a way to get a copy of that book."

Mackay's eyes narrowed and her pointy ears stood almost straight out from her head. "Going home? Who said anything about me going home? Go home indeed! I came here to see the castle, and I *want* to see the castle," she demanded like a spoiled child, her fairy fire burning a bright red. Without a second thought, she shot out the window like a tiny rocket.

"Humans," she said clicking her tongue, "I'm finally free, by the fairy king's braided beard, and I'm not going to be treated like a slave. I may do as I fairy-well please!" As she flew, her words came so quickly they sounded more like the trills of a flute.

Still holding the book, Ella was the first to push her way out of the car while the others fumbled to undo their seat belts. "Mackay! Come on, don't be like that." Ella's words trailed after the fairy who had almost reached the bus stop opposite the library.

As Ella ran toward the enclosure a piercing *skreeeeea* split the sky. Mackay stopped as if she had struck an invisible wall. She hovered there, a few feet out into the road, searching the sky for the source of the cry.

"Hawks!" cried Mackay pointing in terror.

CHAPTER 5

Look to the Skies

FOLLOWING MACKAY'S GAZE, ALL EYES looked skyward as fifteen golden brown hawks swooped down from the clouds. The family watched motionless as Mackay shot through the sky like a comet with a long tail of blue fire blazing behind her.

"Go, Mackay, go," yelled Ella, running with the determination of a child trying to get to home plate before the ball reaches the catcher. Ella had all her attention on the skies and did not see the curb when she reached it. When her front foot sank the extra six inches needed to plant firmly on the road, she stumbled. Though she managed to keep herself from tumbling to the ground, she bent over to clutch her ankle. Fortunately, she had only jarred it. The instant she bent over, a brown feathery blur shot past the spot where her head should have been and curled black talons slashed the air instead of her face.

"Ella, watch out!" screamed Patty from the car. Each time she opened the door and attempted a rescue, she was attacked. The hawks circled overhead, glaring at their prey, while each waited for its turn. One by one the birds dropped with an ear-piercing screech and their talons unfurled. The first few times she had tried to get out of the car, she had swung her purse like a weapon, but the crazed birds had responded with a full-out assault. Snapping beaks thrusting into the half-open windows, slapping wings beating against the doors and roof, talons slashing at any exposed skin, on every side the birds came at once. Patty and Carey and Lili huddled together in the center of the car.

Ella raised the book over her head and hoped for a little protection if the hawk attempted another pass. *Where is Mackay?* she thought. She realized she could not see the little figure anywhere. Though she tried to look everywhere at once, all her attempts to locate the fairy were lost the moment a hawk screeched overhead and dove for another attack.

Ella ran. She knew there were times to stand bravely, but she figured at that moment she could settle for a forced retreat. Her heart was pounding through her chest as she leaped through the doorway into the small plexi-glass room that was the bus stop. As she thudded to the sidewalk she heard sharp talons scratching across the plastic walls as the hawk swooped past the doorway.

For a few moments Ella simply lay on the concrete slab catching her breath. It took all her will power to calm her breathing and clear her mind. She could hear the car door opening and closing as her mother tried to reach her, but the determined hawks kept her at bay.

"Where's Mackay?" Ella asked herself as she rolled over and crawled close to the front wall of the bus stop. With her head on the sidewalk, she peeked through the few inches on the bottom that were not covered by an advertisement for the new play at the Temple Theater. The angle was strange. It's not often that someone looks up and down a city street while lying on the sidewalk, but if she pressed her face against the glass hard enough she could see quite a lot. From what she could see, it looked like the hawk was content to circle around and wait for her to poke her head out again. That was the last thing she intended to do—that was for sure. Though she searched the road and all the trees and lampposts nearby, she could not see Mackay, not even a glimmer of fairy fire. "Please don't let those hawks get Mackay," Ella whispered.

Ella was just beginning to lose hope when she spied a dim blue light shining like a lone Christmas tree bulb. It blinked in one of the openings in the library's rooftop turret. Four more hawks were circling around this round tower that held the library's front entrance. The little blue light kept dancing from window frame to window frame as the hawks flapped their wings and attacked from all sides.

"What am I going to do?" Ella asked herself, clenching her skinned-up hands into fists. She was determined not to cry. "Think, think, think," she said, tapping her forehead with her fingertips as if punctuating each word. "The book!" Ella cried suddenly. Getting up from the ground and grabbing it from the bench it had landed on, she began flipping through the pages. She sat on the bench and rubbed her sore knee as she considered her options. Sitting there with her head tilted, she kept brushing back the stray hairs that had fallen out of her ponytail so they would stop hanging in her face.

"Garden gnomes, no, talking mice, no, captured princesses... definitely not! Come on," Ella growled as she flipped the pages two at a time. "Dragons...that's it!" she said as she stopped at an illustration of four oriental dragons flying around a small girl who was shining like a star. "Well, here we go. I sure hope this works," Ella said crossing her fingers.

Ella concentrated. Forcing out the sounds of hawks and silencing her worries about Mackay, she focused on her reading.

"Chang stood amazed. The old monk from the monastery was right, he realized. The jade statue, a little girl holding a star, was giving off a faint greenish glow. As the light from the statue increased, the flames of the fire rose and writhed, stoked by magic. The wind whipped and howled, bending the branches and scattering leaves. As he watched in wonder he noticed that even the water in his bucket swirled into a miniature typhoon as if it were a tiny sea, the miniscule waves crashing over its sides to splash to the ground.

"'The dragons...' Chang spoke in awe as tendrils of earth, water, wind, and fire coalesced. Each of the four elements issued out of the little jade statue and formed majestic dragons before his very eyes. The first to take shape was the dragon of earth, which burst into being like new growth and blooming buds in springtime."

The air surrounding the book began to cool, and the smell of peach blossoms filled the bus shelter. Ella stopped reading, instinctively knowing she had read enough. Above the written page, little white clouds formed and rippled across the surface.

As she watched, each bank of cloud tumbled off the edge and fell to the concrete floor. Within moments they had condensed, and fog covered the ground. The next moment, green shoots were sprouting from the illustrated page, like the beginnings of some enormous plant. Then, as if someone had sped up time itself, Ella watched as these sprouting seedlings grew into supple branches and were joined by tendrils of vines that writhed and twisted together to fill the bus stop with a long sinuous dragon. Its scales were pieces of bark and lichen. Its claws were roots, and its mane resembled something akin to willow branches. It opened its mouth and exhaled. The breath that rushed through its many rows of splintery teeth blasted Ella's face with the earthy scent of the outdoors after a light rain.

Ella's amazement was mixed with a good dose of fear. In the end her curiosity won out, and she reached to touch the creature's long mossy snout. It responded to her kindness with all the affection of a faithful hound dog. Even its grainy face seemed to smile (if a dragon can be said to do so). The green incandescent eyes closed as she petted the tip of its nose, and its chest rumbled with what sounded like the purring of a very large cat.

"I hope you speak English," said Ella under her breath, walking from its head and feeling along its ridged neck. The dragon seemed to understand her intention and bent low. It tucked in its wings and prepared to be mounted like a docile old horse. With a smile and a thrill of excitement, Ella's reluctance vanished. Before she could second-guess any of the crazy plans coursing through her mind, she straddled the creature. There were no reins, so she would have to do her best to hold on. Once she was seated, the dragon attempted a slight flutter of its wings, but the enclosure was too tight. The rush of air stirred a few pieces of litter under the waiting bench and sent pink petals swirling around the bus stop.

"Well, boy—you are a boy, right?" asked Ella. But the dragon gave a humph as if to say, "No, can't you tell?"

"Well, girl then, can you help me? There're some hawks out there troubling my friend and my family. How about we go show them what a dragon can do, huh?" asked Ella, patting the dragon's neck right behind its leafy ears. The kind eyes of the wooden beast shone brightly, and she nodded in agreement to Ella. Without warning, the dragon snaked out of the bus stop and leaped off the ground with a mighty pump of its wings. Ella grabbed the long willow branches that ran down the dragon's neck and formed the ends of its billowing mane. She hoped they would help her stay on.

It had only taken a moment to call the dragon from her

story book, but Ella hoped Mackay was still safe. Once out of the shelter, the dragon hovered above the sidewalk flapping her wings like a giant butterfly floating above a flower. Perched high up on the creature's broad shoulders, Ella scanned the library for a ball of blue fairy fire. It was right where she had last seen it, dancing between the columns supporting the roof of the tower.

"That's where we need to go, girl," Ella said pointing at the tower. "We have to find a way to save that fairy from those hawks."

The dragon gave a nod of agreement and twisted her long neck around to look Ella in the eyes. It was as if the creature could sense her uneasiness. Ella *was* determined, but her palms were sweating as she held the mane, and her knees shook violently with anticipation as they pressed against the dragon's shoulders. The dragon held her gaze with warm luminous eyes, good-natured and eager. You might think a dragon's eyes would burn like brimstone, all that greed and hate flaming up inside him. That might be true of many dragons, but not this one. She was born of earth and her eyes burned with faithfulness and determination. Nature knows its duty. It does its part as the seasons come and go. As they looked at each other, the steady gaze imbued Ella with courage. Now that they understood each other, they could get to the task at hand. Stretching her

neck back to the sky, the dragon bugled from deep in her throat like a bull elk. The blossom wings pumped and lifted them to the sky. Halfway over the library's front lawn Ella laughed into the wind, flinging out her arms like a bird, completely forgetting herself in the moment. (Please excuse her: you will have to agree that if you were riding on the back of a dragon for the first time, you might be a little excited, too.)

The long body of the dragon was just turning upwards, pointing towards the tower, when tawny wings began beating at Ella's face and long talons swiped at her. One of those cruel hooks ripped through her shirt, slicing into her shoulder as she ducked the sudden attack. Ella cried out in shock and sucked in her breath as she felt the searing pain. Enraged, she tried to clutch her shoulder, grip the dragon's mane, and keep from falling to the pavement all at the same time. She fought her tears as the salty droplets clouded her vision. The scratch burned, but it was not too deep. Grinding her teeth and setting her jaw, she scolded herself for forgetting about that hawk. To Ella's credit, she was a fast learner, and now she was more fully aware of just how much danger she was in.

As the enemy hawk flew off to gain the speed necessary for another attack, Ella took the time to assess her situation. If she had learned anything from playing hockey at the park with her friends, it was that a good player must know where her opponents are at all times. No forgetting this time. Four hawks ahead at the tower, and one above, and some behind her. Not easy, but she thought she had an idea. She pulled the willow branches with her left hand and the dragon swooped to the left in obedience.

"I sure hope this works," Ella said to herself.

CHAPTER 6

Hold on Tight

THE DRAGON TURNED AWAY FROM THE library and raced toward the streetlamps and trees that lined the road. When Center Lake had given itself a face lift, it had put in nice streetlights and maple trees to beautify all the refurbished sidewalks. Now there were three fully grown trees between every lamppost in town. It gave the place shade in summer and a brilliant display of color in the fall, and, Ella hoped, an answer to her problem right now. Putting her plan into action, Ella leaned forward and called out to the dragon, "Let's see how fast you can go around those trees, okay, girl?"

The dragon obeyed, increasing the intensity of her wing beats and narrowing her body to pick up speed. "Don't worry,"

Ella cried encouragingly when she noticed the doubtful look on the dragon's face, "I read this in a book!"

    The turning dragon had drawn the lone hawk's attention. Like a bully careening down a steep hill on his new sled, the hawk dove, as if it wanted to send Ella flying off the dragon's back. Moments later Ella felt a blast of air as the hawk blew past her shoulder. It screeched as it missed her. It had miscalculated its attack and was now forced to wheel around and come up from behind. Ella could hear the piercing cries of her pursuer. The hawk was agitated now, reckless and relentless. It beat its wings furiously, mustering all the strength and speed it had at its disposal. The black-tipped beak was now only a few feet behind Ella. It was riding just above and behind them using the powerful rising air circling off the dragon's wings. The hawk was fast, but not fast enough, and it split the sky with a shrill scream. Ella looked over her shoulder and gave the pursuing bird a mocking smile and contemptuous wave. With one last wing beat, the pair hit the tree line on the side of the parking lot and began swerving between lamp posts and trees. The wind made Ella feel like she was racing in a convertible with its top down. Rounding the second tree in a tight curve, she was forced to forget her elation and lay flat on the dragon's neck as leaves slapped at her rippling hair.

"All right, girl, around the last tree, I want you to wheel left with all you've got while I hold on tight," Ella commanded, and then added to herself, "I hope." Gripping the dragon's mane with all her might and locking her legs around its neck, she tried not to think about what she had just said.

Between the last two trees on the block, the dragon gave one last mighty flap of its wings and then pulled them in for the tight turn. As the dragon's speed reduced, the hawk saw its chance. Extending its feet forward, the beast's eight long talons slashed through the air like tiny scimitars, cutting the flapping tail of Ella's shirt to ribbons. Just before the hawk could pull Ella from her perch, the dragon darted to the left. This sent them careening around the last tree. The gust from the sudden motion caught the bird's open wings and slammed it into a nearby limb. With a thump, the bird crumpled to the ground, stunned.

"Gotcha!" hollered Ella. "Great job, girl. Let's go get Mackay." Completing her full turn, the eager dragon shot from the distant side of the parking lot and passed over the family car. Her wing tips were so low they tapped the green roof, and the gusts of wind from her wingbeats rocked the tiny car on its wheels. Lili's mouth hung open, and Carey even ventured to stick her head out the window and stare in amazement at her sister. But now Ella's flight path had drawn the attention of the hawks that had been circling the car like greedy vultures around a dying man in the desert.

"We had better make this fast before those ugly buzzards catch up," Ella said with a pat on the dragon's neck. "You know what to do."

The dragon opened her canopy of wings and rode the up-draft higher and higher. As she picked up altitude, she left a trail of peach blossoms in her wake. At the peak of her ascent the dragon trumpeted. It was as if she was warning Ella to hold on tight. Then she pulled in her wings and dropped like a stone.

The hawks behind them could not match the dragon's speed, and the hawks around the tower were taken completely by surprise. They were too busy thinking about the potential fairy dinner before them to be paying close attention to what was going on around them. The dragon had done her part well. Without the beating of her wings, she had passed as silently as a fish through water. All Ella could hear was the whistle of the wind in her ears; all she could feel was her stomach in her throat.

Ella closed her eyes as she anticipated the collision. They were within ten feet of the hawks. Like two mighty protective arms, the dragon tucked her wings around Ella's body, and the next instant she rammed the unsuspecting hawks. As she did, she barrel-rolled around the tower. The force of her impact sent the hawks tumbling through the air like pins crashed by a bowling ball. When they pulled out of the tight turn, the dragon opened her wings and Ella was free to survey the damage. All that remained was a cloud of feathers.

Seeing the utter destruction of their comrades, the four remaining hawks stopped their attack. Now they watched as they cautiously circled in the up drafts.

There was no time to waste. The dragon came straight on, charging her enemies. At the last moment she stopped abruptly and reared up like a kicking war horse. Clawing at the air with her long wooden talons, she hovered a few feet away. With green eyes glowing, she gave a mighty roar that sounded like the groaning of a giant oak tree in a storm. With distressed flaps, the hawks turned tail and flew west, beating a hasty retreat. Even under the influence of Aphina's powerful magic, they had no chance of winning. They left as fast as the tailwind could carry them. The battle was over.

"Woohoo! Yeahhhh!" cried Ella, pumping her fists in the air. Then she stopped herself. She had just remembered that she was in the middle of downtown on the back of a dragon.

"That'll show those hawks. By the fairy tree, that was amazing!" proclaimed a tiny voice. Mackay's beautiful face was dripping sweat, and her flower dress was covered in dust from her hiding place, but she did not seem injured by the ordeal. She smiled excitedly and burned with a yellow flame, until she saw Ella's scowl. Seeing Ella's displeasure her radiance changed to a shy, purplish blue.

"What do I say?" Mackay asked sheepishly. "I guess I should apologize…"

But Ella held up her hand to silence her. This was not the time and place for confessions. "Let me say good-bye to this dragon first and then we can talk someplace without spying eyes." The way Ella said it, Mackay knew she meant business.

"Down there, girl, where we came from," said Ella, pointing at the bus stop. Quickly the dragon landed on the sidewalk and crawled inside the shelter. It was hard to believe the whole adventure had taken only a matter of minutes. Ella was just dismounting with wobbly legs when Patty, Carey, and Lili ran up to the doorway.

"Are you all right?" asked Patty, grabbing her daughter by the arm. She hugged her tightly then held her at arm's length to inspect her. That was when she noticed her torn t-shirt and said, "Ella, look at your shoulder!"

"It's just a scratch, Mom," protested Ella, as she tried not to wince when her mother touched it.

"That was so awesome!" cried Lili with a high-pitched squeal. Wide-eyed, she asked, "May I touch him?" Without waiting for an answer from her sister, Lili reached out her hand to pat the dragon's neck and moved to scratch behind her ears.

"I thought you were going to die!" Carey exclaimed. "Ella, did that *really* come out of the book?" She was reeling from the shock, but was straining to notice every last detail of this fantastic creature. It is not every day that someone gets to see a dragon alive and in person, and Carey wanted to remember everything. She wanted to store up every last detail so that she could remember it all when she drew it in her sketch book.

Patty had pulled a handkerchief and small water bottle out of her purse and was cleaning Ella's scratches. "We had better end her story before anyone comes snooping around," she said. "Who knows who saw all that."

"Lili, it's a girl," corrected Ella, trying to ignore her mother. She hoped she could delay the dragon's return, at least for a few more moments. "She told me so herself, sort of."

"She can talk?" asked Lili, a bit stunned.

"Well, no, but she's smart and can understand what I say," answered Ella, giving the dragon a pat on the head. The dragon's wooden face cracked into a splintery grin.

"See?" Ella added.

"Thank you, Miss Dragon, but it's time to go home now," Patty insisted as she handed Ella the storybook. She squeezed her daughter's sweaty hand, raised her eyebrows, and looked pointedly into Ella's eyes.

"Okay, okay," Ella said as she opened the book. Reluctantly she read the last part of the story.

"*Chang placed the jade statue in the monk's hands with a deep bow. 'I have learned the truth. I am content. The dragon stone rightfully belongs to you, wise one. Please keep it.'*

"*The monk bowed his shaven head and returned his orange sash to its proper place on his shoulder. Before he walked away, he offered Chang a few words of wisdom: 'Be not afraid of growing slowly, my son. Be afraid only of standing still.'*

"*Chang considered the proverb, turning the thought around in his mind like meat in a bowl of rice. He watched as the monk's small old figure disappeared over the hill. Finally, he said to himself, I can go home and be at peace. The end.*"

As the words faded, Lili tried to hold onto the dragon's neck. She hoped somehow to keep her from returning to her story, but no matter how hard she squeezed, the wood still transformed into smoke. The dragon barked a final good-bye. Each leaf and branch withdrew. Every blossom and flower closed as they turned to mist and sank into the open page. All that was left was the scent of earth that follows a cloudburst.

When the smoke had faded, everyone looked at Mackay. Her head was down. Her wings were drooping. She sat on the large metal bench with her legs dangling in space as her body glowed with a purple light.

"Mackay, if we're going to help you, you'll have to obey," said Patty sternly, but tempered with a hint of compassion.

"I'm sorry. I've been as stubborn as a troll," Mackay confessed in a mutter. She was reluctant to speak out loud, for even in confession, fairies are proud creatures. Jumping off the bench, Mackay flapped her wings and brought her tiny face as close as she could to the end of Ella's nose. It made it difficult for Ella to see her without crossing her eyes.

Raising one hand with two fingers extended and placing the other over her heart, Mackay pledged, "Thank you. I owe you a life debt. I'll be helpful on your quest from now on. By my honor. That is the way we fairies take an oath." She shook the finger that Ella had stretched out to seal the agreement. "Even *if* you people in Mitch-a-gun are strange," Mackay added under her breath.

Now that the formalities were out of the way, it was time for everyone to walk back to the car as if nothing odd had happened, which meant they all walked in such a way as to look quite guilty of something. Fortunately, no bystanders had seen or heard the last part of their adventure. This is just the sort of luck people have in these kinds of stories.

Once they were all in the car and her mother had started the engine, Carey asked, "Now what?"

"Well," said Patty, thumping her thumbs on the steering wheel, "I guess we're going to have to figure out where Aphina is and what she's up to so we can get the pages back."

"She's probably safely tucked away in some secret place, waiting to cause some kind of trouble. That's what she's always doing back in Frey," said Mackay as she switched the radio on while spinning the radio's tuner knob.

"Mackay, you didn't tell us that you knew anything about Aphina," said Carey as she moved the little fairy away from the radio and turned it off again.

"I said I didn't want to talk about Aphina, not that I didn't know about her. Besides, you didn't ask," answered Mackay with an impish smile and a shrug.

"Do you have anything else you might tell us that could be helpful?" asked Patty, trying to be patient.

"I think Aphina is probably west of here in some dense

forest," confessed Mackay. "Unless there is another castle around here for her to hide in."

"Why west?" asked Lili, pointing east.

"That's east, Lili. That way's west," corrected Ella, pointing out the other window. "Yeah, why west?"

"Because that's the way the hawks went after the fight. Aphina's minions always have to report after a mission," Mackay said, matter-of-factly.

"We have a map at home, Mom. Maybe that will help," suggested Carey.

"Going home *is* the best idea. At least that way we can get the things we'll need," said Patty. "When we get there, we can have a little something to eat. Everyone thinks better on a full stomach. Without me knowing where Aphina is, it's probably not safe for me to leave you all at home alone. We'll have to do this together. Once we've eaten, we can talk over our options, get out that map, and decide what we'll need to pack."

With that decided, everyone buckled up, and the little car drove out of the parking lot headed for home.

CHAPTER 7

The Lake

 WO O'CLOCK. THE LAST TWO HOURS HAD been filled with lots of thinking and discussing. This particular war council had been held over home-made pickles and grilled cheese sandwiches. During the meal it was finally decided that since Lake Michigan and Torch Lake were only a short distance west of their home, and because these large bodies of water would be difficult for Aphina to cross, it only made sense that the remote and wooded parks near these lakes would be her most likely hiding places. Everyone had the opportunity to voice their opinions, and they listened to everything that Mackay could tell them about Aphina. Even with her help, there was no practical way to know which park she was hiding in. In the

end, they used the scientific method of *eenie-meenie-miny-mo* to decide where to search first. When Patty had finished the nursery rhyme, her finger rested on the spot on the map that read South Island, a chip of land lying just off the shores of Price Nature Reserve. Though no one knew it at the time, something greater than fate was working to guide that finger to its resting place. Reader, mark it down. Many roads, seemingly taken at random, have a way of leading us to things that are quite providential. It is strange how life works out in the end.

While they were packing their bags and grabbing their camping gear, it occurred to Patty that those two spots *were* ideal locations for someone to hide. In fact, she was a bit shocked she had not thought of them earlier. As the crow flies, the locations were not that far from their house, and since Aphina appeared to have no concept of or concern for property rights, the trip tromping through people's backyards and woods would not have taken her that long. Thinking it over, Patty also knew that once Burns Park opened up in early summer, South Island and the derelict reserve beside it, with its rough hiking trails, were relegated to nothing but a well-kept local secret. All the tourists would be on the big lake. Without a doubt these places provided the best possible hiding spots in their area. And from what Mackay had told them, these spots would be just the kinds of places that Aphina liked.

Packing for the trip was a cinch. This family loved the great outdoors, and most of the supplies were kept ready for any spontaneous camping trip Dad might spring on the family after coming home from one of his long business trips. After weeks away, he loved escaping with his family out in nature. Once the sleeping bags, backpacks, camping gear, and cooler were stuffed in the car, with the kids crammed in the leftover space, the only thing left for Patty to do was lock the house. With an overloaded car and determined hearts, they headed out on the next leg of their adventure.

In minutes, their little green car was almost to the Eastport landing. It was just a matter of zipping up and down a few hills and fighting the urge to stop at Unger's Orchard and Farmer's Market. This was harder to do than one might think, since there were not only signs dotting the green lawn in front of his farm advertising delicious fresh donuts, tasty homemade cherry pies, and perfect cold cider, but also the tantalizing smells of these foods wafting on the breeze and into the open car windows. When they finally did crest the last hill, they saw the village sign board that was shaped like a blue rowboat and emblazoned with red cursive letters that read, *EASTPORT—Where*

The Lakes Meet You. Patty never could figure out what that was supposed to mean. They passed two or three houses and a little white church before they took their turn. The car tires crunched and the stones made popping sounds as they turned off the main road and onto the gravel one that would lead them to the north landing of Torch Lake.

The locals considered the landing part of the town, if it could be called a town. Eastport was really just a junction on two main roads. In the beginning, twenty families had misguidedly built their houses too close together, and then someone must have gotten the idea of giving the place a name. Most people would not even know it was a town if they had not put up the sign boards.

In fact, back on its two paved side streets, there was nothing but a few closed shops mixed among the houses. In the whole jumble of buildings, there was only one store worth talking about—well, at least the only one not boarded up before Memorial Day and after Labor Day. That was Bud's Grocery, a gas station-slash-grocery store. The locals said it had the 'best greasy fried chicken' in the county. Had it not been for the lakes and the gas station, most people would have left the little town long, long ago.

"Mom, did we have to come to the north side of the lake?

It'll take us over an hour to get to South Island from here," asked Ella as the car parked beside a few hedges in desperate need of trimming. The bulging, unkempt bushes made up the wall that surrounded the landing's parking lot.

"I know kiddo, but remember what I told you at the house? The lake's not so busy up here. Plus, Frank owes me a favor. We can use his boat for up to a week without having to rent it," Patty said, turning off the car. "You girls start unloading the car while I go talk to Frank."

Patty crunched across the gravel to the single-story building. It was a log-sided cabin, painted bright white, with a small, partially lit-up neon sign on the wall. The sign was supposed to read, "Live Bait," but one "i" was winking. So, every other moment it read, "Live Ba t." The window in the store's door was covered with stickers for fishing lures, Chevy trucks, and Michigan Lottery tickets. Patty opened the door and a little bell jingled to announce her arrival.

"Hey, Frank," Patty greeted the owner, a man of early retirement age. Frank was wearing a ball cap of hunter's orange camouflage and his wispy gray hair was coming out the bottom like steam boiling out of a kettle. He looked up from the fly he was tying as he stood behind a pea-green laminate countertop. This was his office, where he sold live bait and fishing licenses, and where he kept his jumbled stacks of paperwork for boat rentals.

"Hello, Patty. Got the boat ready. You guys sure picked a good day for goin' to the island, eh? Lake's as calm as glass, and the fudgies are all down state or over at Burns," said Frank. As he spoke, he walked around the counter and passed the old gumball machines that still held candy in them from the 1980s. Once he was in front of the counter he added, "Gas tank's all filled up and everything."

"Thanks, Frank. I really appreciate it."

"No problem, but I do have to tell you guys, one of the oars is broke. I was goin' to go to Charlevoix and get a new one at the hardware store, you know the one on Fifth Street, behind the new Dollar Store? but I hadn't got the chance to yet," Frank explained, while tucking his shirt tail back into his faded jeans. "No-good tourists, not sure they're worth the trouble," he complained with a huff. "You guys won't believe it. Saturday this fudgie comes over, see, and he asks to rent my boat so he and his kids could do some 'bonding.' Pulled in here with his brand spanking new Volvo SUV and eight hundred dollars' worth of fishing equipment, and wants to go out. You know the type. Well, he come back after four hours, red as a radish, and says his bratty kids accidently broke one of my oars

The Lake

playing around. Not sure what they were doin'. Anyways, he hands me a hundred bucks and told me to keep the change. Tourists! Some of 'em think money fixes everything. What a putz!"

"Don't worry about it, Frank. We shouldn't need it," Patty said, as Frank grabbed a package of Twizzlers from the candy aisle and shuffled past Patty and the cash register so he could open the door for her.

"Frank," Patty protested.

"What? Come on, kids need candy. One pack never hurt nobody, eh? Look at me," he said, patting his bulging belly that was padded with twenty pounds of extra love.

"Yeah, I see," Patty laughed.

"Hey guys," Frank said as he stepped onto the creaky wooden dock. The kids were almost done loading the aluminum rowboat.

"Hi, Frank," Carey said as she placed her backpack in the middle of the boat. Patty noticed that hers looked a whole lot heavier than all the rest. Then again, Carey always liked to be overly prepared.

"Hi, Mr. Frank," said Lili, eyes gleaming as she tried not to look at the large bag of Twizzlers Frank held in his right hand.

"Hey Blondie, catch," Frank smiled as he threw the candy to the eight year-old. "Make sure you guys share 'em."

"Yes, sir," said Lili with a toothy grin after catching the bag. Like a greedy squirrel hiding nuts, she quickly unzipped her bag and tried to cram the Twizzlers into the already-stuffed pocket on the front of her backpack.

Frank shuffled over to the end of the dock where the boat was tied up. He peered down and gave everything one final check. He wanted to make sure he had not forgotten anything. For a gruff independent old bachelor, Frank really was one of the nicest people a person could ever meet. "Everything looks fine. Remember the engine is a little fussy if you give it too much gas," Frank explained as he gave one of Ella's braids a friendly tug as she walked past him and stepped into the boat. "Well, you guys have fun, eh?"

"Thanks again, Frank," said Patty one last time. With a smile, Frank turned and headed back to the shop.

"By the way," Frank turned as he reached the end of the dock, "Patty, make sure Blondie there doesn't get all excited and start feeding the lake gulls. I heard about some lady getting attacked by some birds earlier this morning at Frisk's roadside stand in Atwood. You know how the gulls get, once those dumb city folks start givin' 'em food. Once that starts, they start badgerin' everybody."

"Who? Me?" Lili laughed at the accusation. She lifted her empty hands in an attempted gesture of innocence.

Frank pointed his knobby calloused finger at her like the barrel of a gun. "Yeah you, sport!"

"Okay, okay, no feeding the animals," Lili finally conceded with a grin.

"Have fun," Frank said again as he waved his free hand. His other hand was stuffed deep into the pocket of his jeans trying to fish out his last stick of chewing gum.

"Phew, I thought that man would never leave," said Mackay, popping out of the folds of a sleeping bag a few moments later. "I still don't understand why you people in Mitch-a-gun don't believe in fairies. It's all very barbaric," Mackay complained while dusting off her new traveling clothes. She had made them out of daisies and leaves during the last hour of the family's preparations. When she had presented herself at the car, she was burning brightly, and the flames were as orange as a ripe tangerine.

"You know the rules, Mackay!" Ella said as she walked up and down the dock to make sure everything was balanced and packed properly in the boat. "You know you have to hide when strangers are around so they don't see you."

"Mom, I can't get this life jacket thingy to buckle up," complained Lili as she fumbled with the white plastic clips on her life vest.

"Come here." Patty bent down to help her youngest daughter and noticed the unspoken concern in Lili's big brown eyes. She squatted there for a few moments and just looked at her. Their eyes met. Lili's face was a mask of calm, but Patty could tell that the emotions hidden inside were running like a herd of wild horses. She had learned over the last few years how important it was to pay attention to her children. They *were* people after all.

"Out with it, Lili-Lou," Patty said gently, "What's bothering you?"

Lili leaned in, rubbing her mother's hand between her forefinger and thumb the way she always did when she felt uncomfortable. "I'm scared a little," Lili confessed, trying to look more confident than she felt. "I mean, up 'til now I've been excited, almost as if everything was just a big game, but in the car, I started thinking. What if..."

Lili trailed off.

"If we're always worried about tomorrow, we'll never live

today, girlie," Patty said. She cupped her daughter's cheek with her hand. "Baby girl, there will always be *what-ifs*."

"I know, Mom, but once I started thinking about Aphina I got all scared. She makes me so afraid," Lili said, her shoulders trembling despite the heat.

"I know, Lili, this whole thing can be scary," Patty said lifting the tiny chin that had fallen in shame, "but what does your father tell you to do when you're afraid?"

"Think truth," Lili quoted.

"That's right. When you are afraid, think truth, because the truth has nothing to be afraid of." Patty said, punctuating her words with a tender kiss to Lili's forehead. "Remember, truth always wins in the end."

Patty watched the words sink into Lili's soul. She saw the light of truth fighting for control of her heart and mind. The black clouds of doubt that were threatening, seeking to crowd out the hope in those brown eyes, suddenly parted. Lili's face was aglow with happy sunshine, like a clear blue summer's sky that has had its face washed with a sudden cloud burst. Fears dispelled, Lili gripped her mother in an intense hug. Patty stood up and stretched her legs. Taking inventory, she saw that Ella was in the boat with Mackay buzzing around her head like a house fly around a plate of food. *But where's Carey?* she wondered. She looked up the dock and into the parking lot. Next to the car, she saw Carey locking up the Bug.

"Ella, you start the motor. Remember to turn it on before you pull the cord or you'll flood the engine," Patty said. "I'll be right back." She headed over to join Carey.

Patty stepped off the wobbly dock and crossed the gravel lot. Carey was picking up her mother's backpack to take it to the boat. Patty watched her daughter, wondering how thirteen years had flown by and when she'd gotten so grown up. The girl was getting to be all legs and was nearly as tall as Patty. Carey's long blonde hair and tan skin were striking, too. People had started joking with her father on a regular basis, saying that if his girls got any more beautiful, he'd have to buy a shotgun to keep the boys away. Fortunately, Carey had no idea how pretty she was.

"I got it, Carey," Patty said, taking the backpack from her daughter. "Thanks for all your help, kiddo. You know I really appreciate how much I can count on you."

"Thanks," Carey replied, giving that straight thin smile she gave when her mind was really someplace else. Suddenly she gripped Patty's free hand and squeezed it, stopping and anchoring them to that spot before they walked the rest of the way to the dock. "Mom, can I tell you something while the girls are in the boat?"

"Sure, Carey-bird, what's up?" Patty adjusted her backpack on her shoulder.

"I was just thinking..." Carey paused, looking down at the ground. She kicked a loose piece of gravel before she started talking again. "I'm not sure I'm ready for this."

"This what?" asked Patty. She knew questions always helped Carey when she was struggling with her thoughts.

"This—this adventure. I'm not sure I'm ready for it. I've been reading books all my life. Making up stories in my head. Dreaming about swooping in to save the day or being saved myself. But those were just daydreams. This is real. What I do here counts for something, has consequences. I mean, what if I make a wrong decision, or freeze, or mess up and destroy everything?" Carey's worries tumbled out and the corners of her eyes brimmed with unshed tears.

Patty placed her hands on her daughter's shoulders and turned her to face her. She tilted her head up so she could look her in the eyes. Those eyes were normally the color of a bright blue sky, but right now they were gloomy with gray clouds of doubt.

"Carey, I know you worry, but you have been given

responsibility your whole life. When the time comes, if it comes, you will know what to do. Besides, those stories won't be wasted. You'll see. I think all good stories are a training ground. They are a safe place to learn from other people's decisions. And you never know, maybe an idea from one might just come in handy, after all."

"But what if I make a mistake?" Carey whispered.

"Carey, only one person has never made a mistake. When you have to make a choice in a crisis, it's not so much about making decisions, but following the truths you already know. Go where they point you."

"You really think I can do this?" asked Carey, placing her chin on her mother's shoulder and hugging her.

"You are braver than you believe, stronger than you seem," she began the familiar quote, and Carey joined in on the last part: "and smarter than you think."

Patty hugged her daughter back until she let go and hefted her backpack again.

"I love that quote," whispered Carey.

"I know. Ready to go?"

"Yeah, Mom. Thanks."

In just a few moments, the group was settled and the boat was puttering along the smooth surface of the lake. Frank had

The Lake

been right. Torch Lake was deserted. Their boat was the only thing disturbing the clear, almost tropical-blue water, and the only sounds to be heard were the sputters of the boat motor and the cries of the lake gulls.

As captain, Patty manned the little powder-blue engine. The older two girls, as officers, were in charge of cargo, so they sat beside the bags, backpacks, and cooler packed around the middle two seats. Last of all were the two recruits, Lili and Mackay, who were left to stretch out over the prow of the boat like two carved maidens on an old wooden ship. As the boat scooted along, Mackay could not contain herself. The excitement of being so close to this much water was just too much for her to handle. She would lean out, then she would start wiggling, then she would jump over the side of the boat like an Olympic high diver, swooping down so that she could fly, skimming along the lake's surface like a wild dragonfly. As she went along, she would peer through the rippling water, hoping to see a fish. Luckily for her she did not, as she looked an awful lot like something a nice big pike would like to eat.

After about ten minutes, Mackay suddenly zipped up from the surface of the lake and popped up in front of Patty, interrupting a conversation she and Ella were having about the weather.

"When're we gonna get there?" Mackay asked.

"About an hour," answered Patty.

"What's an hour?" Mackay scrunched up her face and scratched her head.

"Probably a very long time for a fairy," answered Patty, "but don't worry Mackay. If you're patient, we'll be there before you know it."

"Patient," Mackay said, tasting the word as if it was mildly unpleasant, "You know, we don't have a word for that in Fairie."

"Why am I not surprised?" Carey whispered to Ella.

"Well, if you can't get that steel oar thingy to move faster, I guess I will just sleep a little. All this sitting around is making me tired," said Mackay as she stretched out her arms and yawned.

"That's probably a good idea," Patty said.

After Mackay fell asleep, everyone else fell into talking and looking at South Island as they drew closer. The conversation made time pass quickly, and in a little less than an hour they were almost there. The plan was simple. After a quick pass around the island, they could moor their boat at the dock and set up camp at the forest reserve.

South Island was no more than a hump of land about a hundred feet in diameter with a few birch and pine trees surrounded by grass and large stones. It was nothing much to look at and definitely would not take long to search. It did have two underwater sand bars that jutted out to west and east like the claws on a mossy crab. They formed a little cove on one end of the island. Inside the boundaries of this sandy little reef the water was only two or three feet deep, depending on where a person was standing. Sometimes in the middle of the summer, the locals would park their boats inside the sand bar arms and use the shallows for their "beach parties." The best part about the whole place was the fact that outside the sandbars, the lake bottom just dropped off—almost fifty feet straight down. It was a great place for swimming, but it appeared that there was no one around today.

Since the plan was to park their boat at the dock at Price Nature Reserve, Patty turned the tiller to navigate around the little island. Floating past the island would be enough to see if Aphina was around. Though her intentions were simple enough, Patty had no idea there was a plan already working to frustrate her efforts.

CHAPTER 8

South Island

EADER, IF YOU ALLOW, I WILL TRY TO explain. Hours before, Ella had quite innocently placed the sparkling crow's feather into a loop of her backpack as a decoration. You will have to forgive her, as she was unacquainted with Aphina's deceitful ways. She did not know that Aphina would never be so foolish as to have left that feather by accident. Ella had packed it because she had no way of suspecting the truth. Aphina had planted that feather. She had sprinkled it, you remember, with white Eyra Dust, and that, mixed with the Night Shade, allowed her to hear anything said close by. All this while, Aphina had been spying on them.

Right at that moment, somewhere in the reserve, Aphina

was pulling a black mantle over her head like a hood. Her eyes and nostrils filled with the smoke from the fire that was smoldering in front of her. In her hands she held a bowl one of her new minions had stolen for her. She had no idea where it had come from, but that mattered little. Now that it was filled with water, she knew what she would do with it.

Her eyes tried to focus through the smoke as she stared at her reflection in the water. With a wave of her hand she shushed the servile animals that were gathered around her, even her pet crow. *I need to concentrate,* she thought. Finally, all was quiet. She allowed her anger to boil as she listened to the family, letting their happy conversation feed her bitterness. Quietly, she began to mumble words that danced to a rhythm, and she moved her fingertips on the surface of the water.

Back on the lake, the sun was shining and the breeze was soft, when without warning, the water began to rise and fall like water in a bath tub where a child is playing instead of bathing. Everyone in the little boat grabbed for handholds as it bobbed like a cork.

"Hold on," Patty shouted as the motor tried to push them through the choppy waves.

"Mom, what's going on?" asked Ella.

"I don't know. There's no wind," Patty answered as the waves smacked into the sides, making the thin aluminum reverberate with hollow thumps and splashing water into the bottom of the boat. By this time, the boat was cresting over little swells and the engine was sputtering as it cut through larger waves. A small spray of water doused Mackay as she slept on a bag.

"Hey, who's splashing?" she complained sleepily, her wild curls matted on one side of her head from sleeping on them.

"It was the lake," said Lili as she gripped the bow of the ship with both hands. She looked a little green around the gills. She was trying her very best not to think about all the swaying back and forth. Mackay noticed that Carey and Ella were busy bailing water out of the bottom of the boat with the two little pails Frank had left for customers to put bait in. The waves were coming in giant five-foot swells now, the surface of the water pitching up and down violently. The little boat could not cut through the rough water like a speed boat, so they had to crest every wave as it attacked them.

"Mom, what are we going to do?" asked Carey, with a worried glance at her mother.

"You guys keep bailing, and I am going to try to get us to the sand bar on the right. The water looks smoother over there. Dad took me swimming here last summer, and the water over the whole thing is only a few feet deep. I'm thinking the sand bar should break the waves, but you guys will have to help me. Got it?" Patty said.

The girls willed the boat forward. Lili even rocked back and forth in her seat as if that might help push them through the raging water. Suddenly the water's motion changed. Before, the waves were coming at all angles as if being thrashed about by some giant unseen hand, now they calmed for the briefest of moments. As the family looked about in wonder, they noticed that the water behind them began to spin ever so slowly. As the waters changed course, the waves crashed into each other, sending splashes and spray flying through the air. In a few seconds the lake was churning. They were almost to the sandbar now, just a matter of a few feet, but the pulling, grasping water caused the motor to strain to keep them on course. The water behind them was a whirling vortex, the waves rippling into seething strands of blue and white, much like the pattern of a pinwheel as it spins around. The air about them began to roar with the sound of rushing water. As Carey bailed water out of their boat, her little bucket was ripped out of her hands by the increasing speed of the pulling waves. She watched as it was swept away from sight into the mass of swirling water. The five inches sloshing in the bottom of the boat helped them as they reached the edge of the sand bar. The added weight pressed into the sandbar just a few inches below the surface, and they felt it scraping as they passed over its edge and into the shallow water beyond. The motor sputtered and puffs of black smoke came out of the exhaust like rings from a pipe. It shuddered one last time and died, as if the black smoke had been its soul, departing from its worn-out body.

"It overheated," Patty shouted as the churning swells grabbed at them and tried to pull them back into open water. Fortunately, the sandbars slowed the power of the waves, and the water struggled to control them. For a moment or two, the boat coasted forward with the remaining momentum from the dead motor, then they stopped. The whole boat stood still for a few seconds, and then it began to inch backwards toward the lake. Patty was not sure what to do.

"Mom, we've got to get out of here before those waves pull us back into deep water!" Ella sounded a bit panicked.

Carey's eyes brightened with an idea, while her mother tried to restart the motor.

"Mom, the oars! The water's not deep here. We can use them like the poles of a gondola." Carey grabbed the whole oar and handed it to her mother as she used the broken one on her side.

"Ella, you keep bailing so we don't sink," Patty commanded.

"Carey, you push on the right side so the waves don't suck us out into open water." Holding her oar firmly, she started counting, "One, two, push!"

Patty and Carey strained on their oars like slaves in a galley ship. The waves hitting the boat sounded like the beating of a drum. Slowly they were rewarded, as the boat moved a few feet towards shore. They were grateful that the sand bar hidden right below them helped to deaden the strength of the current and waves. Their progress was ever so slow, but thankfully, reader, even the slightest progress will breed hope in your heart when you are in great peril.

"Keep pushing, Carey! We're not far now." Patty encouraged her daughter as their muscles began to burn with the effort.

Lili had placed Mackay in her shirt pocket and was holding on for dear life. Mackay's wings had gotten wet and there was no way for her to fly. Lili felt there was nothing else that she could do. She was too afraid to think of helping her sister, so she just sat there staring at Ella, who was bailing water out of the boat.

Fortunately for our family, Aphina had exhausted most of the water in her bowl, and there was a limited supply in her hiding place. She was reduced to vigorously swirling the last inch or so of water about, since most of it had sloshed onto the ground.

"Why are you so persistent?" Aphina hissed.

Despite Aphina's efforts, the boat drew closer to the island. The twenty yards they had traveled had taken most of their strength. Patty's and Carey's arms felt like stretched-out rubber bands. Though everything in their upper bodies cried for rest, they could not stop. The waves, like long foaming fingers, were tearing at them, trying to pull the boat out of the shallows. Each one was hoping to snatch, grasp, or pry. Maybe *it* would be the one to pull them back into the deep water. Leaning into the work, Patty and Carey had their oars six inches deep in sand, fighting the undertow. Just when Carey thought she could not go on, the swirling water slowed. The momentary lull gave them hope to try one last thrust. Without warning, the water rose up in a giant wave in one final assault. It was a wall of water coming after them. Its white foaming top collapsing into a torrent of bubbles and spray, hoping to sink them or at least hurl them out of the boat and into the water.

"Push!" Patty cried.

The wave was too late. The power of its attack was now at their back. All it did was help to propel them onto South Island beach. Coming up hard, the aluminum bottom reverberated with the sounds of metal scraping along sand and gravel as the boat skidded to shore between two large rocks. They were stuck fast, three-quarters of the boat firmly on land, while the waves continued to thump the back side of the boat.

All four passengers jumped overboard and onto the beach. Gripping the bow, they pulled, tugging the boat all of the way on shore. The waves abruptly stopped. In a matter of seconds, the lake had returned to a glassy calm, as if nothing had happened. The still water and clear weather matched, as they should. The girls gawked, dumbfounded. Lili knelt down and kissed the ground as Carey collapsed, exhausted. "Dry ground," Lili exclaimed, and gave a large boulder a huge hug and an extra kiss, her words accompanied by the smack of her lips on the stone.

"Was that Aphina?" asked Ella. She was taking shallow breaths and doing all she could not to think about her nauseated stomach. She sat on the sand, closed her eyes, and leaned the side of her head against the boat. She just wanted to stop all the sloshing.

"I don't know what else it could be," Patty said, "but it looks like it's over." She looked across the calm water as she sat down on the beach to rest. As she sat there thinking, a chill ran down

her spine, prickling her flesh and giving her the shudders. It was as if she could feel Aphina watching them that very moment.

After a few minutes of catching their breaths and calming their stomachs, Patty was the first to speak. "Well, no point sitting around here all day. I think we can safely say that Aphina's not on South Island. I want us to get over to the Reserve to set up camp so we can look around before it gets dark. That way we can make sure the area around our campsite is safe. Tomorrow morning we can start searching. I'm hoping it won't take too long to find her."

"Then what?" asked Carey doubtfully.

"Don't worry. I'm working on that. I have a few ideas, but right now we can't do anything until we find her," Patty said, standing up. She placed her hand on the bow of the boat to steady her shaky legs.

"But Mom, what if…" Lili trailed off as fear clamped down

and choked off her last words. She sat for a moment beside the boat, her eyes wide, like a frightened deer, until her feelings of helplessness turned into frustration. "I mean, come on Mom, Aphina could have killed us."

"Girls—" Patty dusted the sand off her legs. "—I don't have all the answers, but there are times to face our doubts and there are times to silence them. Worrying adds nothing to tomorrow, while it takes away from today. We are going to have to trust one another and cross those bridges as we come to them. All I can tell you for certain is what I was told all the time growing up: 'When you don't know what to do, do what you know to do.' And what I *do* know is that we can't stop at this point. We brought Aphina here. That means we've got to find a way to put her back."

All three girls leaned on the truth and conviction in their mother's words. The words sunk into the dry soil of their hearts like rain in a drought-stricken land. At first they simply sat there thinking, but soon, the truth worked its own magic. They knew their duty. Without a word, each one tightened the ropes that restrained her fears and made the decision that had to be made. One by one each girl stood up, brushed off her clothes, and poured water out of her soggy shoes. Carey first, then Ella, and last, but not least, Lili. They stood resolute. They must move forward.

Patty gave each girl a hug before she started issuing orders. "Okay, Lili and Ella, you two check to see how wet everything is, while Carey and I check out the engine," she said, assigning everyone their tasks.

Twenty minutes later, the entire load had been unpacked, inspected briefly, and repacked. They had discovered that two of the sleeping bags were a bit damp, but besides that, nothing too important had gotten wet.

"Everything looks okay to me, Mom," Ella said, "but I did find something interesting."

"Arghh, come on!" Patty muttered, trying not to slap the side of the engine in frustration. "I opened the throttle, cut the choke, and tried to start the motor, just like I'm supposed to, but it just won't work!" Patty only half heard her daughter. Trying again, she pulled the cord one last time. The engine made a sputtering sound and died, belching out another puff of black smoke. Waving the smoke away from her nose and eyes, Patty stopped working and turned to Ella.

Seeing that she finally had her mother's full attention, Ella started over, "Everything looks fine. Nothing's too wet, but I think I found something. It's the feather, the one we found back at our house. It's not shining anymore. Does that mean Aphina's lost her power or something?" she asked eagerly.

Patty was about to say that she had no idea, when Mackay interrupted her. "Is it wet?" Now that her wings were dry, Mackay was as busy as ever. At this moment she was pushing multiple buttons on the motor.

"Mackay, please don't help. *Is it wet?* Well, water shouldn't hurt the motor." Patty answered. Then she shooed her away from the engine before she could 'fix' anything.

"No, not the metal thing, the feather. Is the feather wet?" Mackay popped up in Ella's face. She was so excited that she was blazing like a small sun, which made it kind of hard for Ella to look at her without seeing spots before her eyes. Twenty minutes of exploring a new island and asking endless questions will do that to a curious fairy.

"Yes, it must've gotten wet when the waves splashed all over everything in the boat. Why?" Ella asked Mackay.

"That's probably why it's not glowing. Night Shade Dust can't stand up to water. That's the reason Aphina doesn't let her pets out in the rain."

"As interesting as all this is," said Carey, who was sitting next to the boat trying to read the engine manual she had found in the box with the safety kit, "if we can't find a way off this island it won't much matter, will it? Unless of course, you think that that feather is going to fly us out of here or get the engine to work," Carey added sarcastically, feeling grumpy and frustrated over the broken motor.

"Carey, your sarcasm really *isn't* appreciated," rebuked Patty with a sigh, but then an idea popped into her mind and she added, "*but* your idea sure is."

Patty got out of the boat and walked over to the three or four things left on shore and opened Ella's backpack. "Ella, the book's in here, right?"

"Yeah, Mom, in the big pocket."

"Lili, Ella, you guys finish loading up the boat, and make sure to arrange everything so that most of the heavy stuff's in the back," ordered Patty.

"If you say so," said Ella and Lili, looking kind of confused.

"Carey, I hope you packed like you normally do. Did you pack a rope?" Patty asked.

"Yes, I figured we might need some."

"Good, please get it out and put half the length through the docking loop on the front of the boat," Patty directed as she opened the book.

"Sure thing, Mom, but *what* are you doing?"

"I thought that if we can't get over the lake by engine, we

might get a few helpers to pull us across," Patty explained, as she began flipping through the book. She stopped at an illustration.

"This should work," Patty said, pointing at a picture of an Indian princess surrounded by beautiful white swans. Each swan had its wings outstretched in flight and looked as if it were dancing around the young woman in the picture. As for the smiling young woman, she was dressed in a purple silk sari embroidered with ornate golden trim and designs that looked like peacock feathers, her wrists and lower arms were covered in golden bangles, and a diamond encrusted ring encircled the raven black tresses of her head like a crown.

"Well, here it goes," Patty said, raising her eyebrows and cocking her head to one side. She hoped this was a good idea. Holding the book out before her, she seated herself on a dry stump at the edge of the sand. She took a few short breaths and tried to clear her mind. She wanted to focus so that she would read clearly and with emotion. She did not know if that would help to achieve her goal, but she figured it surely could not hurt. Then she began to read...

"Princess Manjula wept, and as she did, her tear drops fell one by one onto the green grass. The grass was always lush in her father's secret garden, because it was fed by the Gandak River, which offered its fresh cool waters from the

nearby Himalayan Mountains. The royal engineers had designed it so, and it made the place a paradise. It was in the midst of this secret oasis that she hid. The garden was her refuge. She had learned in childhood that this garden was the one safe place for her to cry. As she cried, the scents of lilies and orchids were carried on the breeze, but they could not seduce her from her quiet contemplations. Today her heart suffered, and the pain was acute. What else could she feel as she gazed at the twelve snow white swans swimming in the pond?

"Each slender graceful neck stretched out and dipped its majestic head into the water. They performed what appeared to be an intricate dance while she watched. Each swan, though a perfect specimen in its flawless form, was marked in one strange way. A mark which revealed a closely guarded family secret, a secret that pricked her heart every time she thought of it. There, perched on the top of each white head, lay a strand of pearls and a large round emerald set in gold. The ringlets atop each head formed twelve small crowns. These crowns were the only things left, besides the grace and beauty of these birds, that spoke of the royal princesses that had been hidden within.

"'Why did that old guru curse my sisters? Why was he so

wicked?' questioned Manjula. She had been forced to watch, one by one, as each of her sisters was transformed into a swan. Each one in her year; each one as she came of marrying age. All because her father had refused to give his eldest daughter to that decrepit low-caste old man. 'And now,' said Manjula speaking to herself in frustration, 'I, the last of my father's beloved children, am cursed to join them. Next week, at the start of my fifteenth year, my life as I know it, will end.'

"Determined, Manjula wiped the tears from her eyes and rose, speaking to herself. 'No, this must not be the end. I still have one week and I must try... even if I meet the curse at the end. I will find a way,' Manjula vowed. Her deep brown eyes simmered with determination as she walked to her palanquin followed by a silent group of servants."

Something told Patty to stop reading. She had read enough. Her words evaporated as the heat of a tropical sun warmed her face. A gust of wind brushed her cheek, carrying the scents of a flourishing royal garden. Patty even thought that she could taste the spicy curry being cooked in the kitchens of a nearby palace.

As she savored this momentary window into Manjula's world, white feathers began to fly out of the illustration on the page. They burst out of the seams of the painting, like the stuffing of a pillow during a wild pillow fight. As each one squeezed into Patty's world, it was caught on the breeze and twirled down to the surface of the lake like a whirling dervish. Once they had all landed, they floated, surrounded momentarily by the ripplets they made on the surface of the water. Then they began to grow, the feathers' shafts extending and bending to form the bodies and necks of the swans. The white barbs of each feather stretched and divided. They multiplied and spread like the opening of a delicate fan and formed majestic white wings. As twelve pairs of wings fluttered, and twelve bodies grew and formed, the twelve quill tips of the feathers bent and curved and created bills and black-masked faces with serene, serious eyes.

"Wow," Ella exclaimed.

"They're so beautiful," said Carey with appreciation.

"I'm glad that worked. I was kind of afraid we would have an Indian princess instead of twelve swans," Patty said.

The swans waddled up on shore and shook out their wings. The largest of the swans approached Patty.

Patty gave a curtsy. "Your majesty."

The swan returned her greeting by ducking her head.

"Now what?" asked Ella.

"Carey and Ella, start making loops in the ropes. We will need twelve. Not too tight, though."

"Oh, I see where you're going," Carey added with a smile.

"And Lili, please try to keep Mackay from disturbing our guests," Patty instructed Lili, as Mackay hovered around the heads of the two smallest swans. She was flapping her arms like wings and was making "too-too" sounds with her pinched lips. She thought she sounded like a trumpet.

"I know how to speak Swan, maybe I can help," Mackay protested as Lili tried to distract her with the job of checking the bags on the boat.

During the time it took to make the twelve loops in Carey's rope, Patty introduced herself and her daughters to the twelve princesses and told them about their circumstances and the help they required. Though the swans could not speak, they were still *real* princesses in spirit, and before the loops were finished, they were lining up on shore. Each stood there trumpeting as she waited for her harness. They seemed more than ready to lend their wings to a good cause.

Carey made sure each slender neck was harnessed and the rope was as close to their bodies as she could manage. Then Patty stationed herself in the middle of the boat to aid as best she could with her one good paddle. The girls sat in the far back to help reduce the load.

"Girls, you try to remain as still as possible. I am hoping that will help make our trip a little faster." To the swans, Patty said, "If you please, your majesties," giving a slight bow.

In unison the majestic white wings beat against the water. Three down beats striking the surface was all each bird needed before being airborne. Patty fought to keep her balance as the boat pulled away from the shore. She strained with every stroke of her oar, trying her very best to help the birds.

"Forget Santa's sleigh, we're being pulled by swans," Carey shouted.

Mackay clapped her hands with joy, as Lili grinned from ear to ear. Ella just sat serenely, looking out at the motion of the birds, with her chin resting on the boat's railing. She looked like she was savoring the memories of a pleasant dream.

After half an hour and two stops to rest the birds, they made it to the shore of the Reserve. Ella and Carey were as polite as possible as they removed the loops from each swan. Acting like a maid servant from a princess movie, Lili approached each one with a curtsy and a proper 'Thank you, your majesty.' After the thanks had been given and the ropes removed, it was time to say goodbye.

The girls lined up according to their ages, and Mackay sat on Patty's shoulder as she read the last words of their story.

"Manjula's father wept for joy, which was not a common occurrence for a Raja. He did not care for his self-respect at this moment. Let them look on if they wish, for who can hide such joy? he thought. The tears ran down his face into his gray, oiled beard while his white turban and fat belly shook with spasms of laughter. After so many years he could now embrace his twelve daughters. They were no longer swans, but women once more.

"Manjula rejoiced as she touched skin and not feathers for the first time in many years. She was no longer alone. She was whole in heart after so many years of emptiness. Then she looked over her father's shoulder at the tall handsome man who had saved her, the man, who in fact, had saved them all. As she looked, she knew. She knew a new story was about to begin. The End."

The story was over, but the power of the words lingered in the air, like the scent of a candle suddenly blown out. Each girl savored the fading pictures in her mind and was left with a simple but deep impression. The swans' bodies dissolved back into feathers which swirled on the breeze, and then fluttered toward the open page as if being gently pulled. The faint echoes of trumpeting birds rang in their ears, and each girl swallowed the lump in her throat and waved goodbye as the final feather landed on the surface of the page and then vanished.

Carey asked sentimentally, "Why is it so hard to say goodbye every time?"

"Isn't that how it is with good books? You always want to savor the last chapter. When you close the cover of a good book, it's like closing a door on a whole world of friends," said Patty.

Everyone sat reverently for a while, even Mackay. Her fairy light shown a sad, contemplative blueish-gray, like a sky on a rainy day. The moment was solemn and made everyone pensive and quiet, until Ella scattered it with a sudden burst of laughter and said, "I'll tell you one story I can't wait to end— Aphina's."

The whole family chuckled at Ella and her mischievous grin, then Patty closed the book.

"Okay, girls, let's go set up camp."

CHAPTER 9

At Camp

THEY SET UP CAMP IN A GREEN CATHEDRAL. Its rafters and beams were made of oak, maple, and beech limbs. Its walls were built of lesser trees: young poplars, myrtles, and ash. Its roof looked like thousands of green stained-glass windowpanes as the afternoon sun shone through the transparent skins of leaves. This dim light cast a warm, sacred glow over the entire clearing. The treetops were filled with the songs of birds, as blue jays and cardinals perched in the branches like gargoyles. A chattering chorus of squirrels completed the song, sitting perched on lower limbs like saints, their little fists clasped around half-eaten nuts. They looked for all the world as if they were praying.

The camp itself was in the shape of a large diamond. The sides of this diamond were made of four fallen logs that had been rolled over to serve as benches. Outside the diamond, on the left and right-hand sides were two larger rocks, sunk waist-deep in the earth. They would serve as tables, which appeared to be the reason they had been left that way in the first place. Right in the middle of all this, they built their fire pit. It was made up of a double ring of small rocks collected from the beach. Once all this hard work was done, the only thing left to do was to pick out where the girls would put their sleeping bags. After a few minutes of debating and bargaining, everything was arranged. In the end, each girl was convinced she had the best place to sleep.

The moments that followed were wonderfully mundane. That might not seem to make sense to some readers, but in the middle of an adventure there is a bit of relief in doing something normal, especially when other moments are filled with such anxiety. Camping was something normal and comfortable. It did not seem strange, like so many other parts of this long day. The girls enjoyed collecting firewood. They enjoyed stopping from time to time to pick wildflowers. They enjoyed skipping stones in the lake. Once all the firewood was collected, Patty even allowed Lili a few whacks at a large log she was chopping for the fire pit. It was so refreshing to laugh and share good-natured jokes.

Ella and Lili, like many fortunate girls and boys, had grown up hearing many fairy tales, and they gave their mother excited hugs when she told them they could play with Mackay while she and Carey started to cook supper. They had always wanted to play with a fairy.

By the time the girls joined the fairy, she had already found an abandoned bird's nest and was setting up a snug little campsite for herself. Lili watched with rapture, giggling from time to time when she thought Mackay had done something funny. She even brayed like a little donkey once, when Mackay had a sneezing fit while sweeping out all the dust. It was hilarious to watch the fairy explode with frustrated red flames every time she dropped her tiny pine-sprig broom to clutch at her nose and sneeze. Ella, on the other hand, drank in every last detail. She sat quietly on a stump and drew scene after scene in a sketch pad she had brought along.

Much later, when the smells of supper wafted over to the little group, Mackay decided it was time she allowed the girls to help. The two girls jumped at the opportunity. They had lots of ideas stored up in their imaginations from hours of dreaming what fairy houses might be like. They helped make a pillow from sleeping bag fiber, a blanket from a few fresh leaves stitched together, and a small water bucket and dipper from a water bottle top and an acorn cap. At the end, all three of them stood back looking over their handy work; one burning with radiant yellow fairy fire, and the other two beaming with contented, happy smiles.

There was an hour or two of daylight still left by the time the younger girls were called to set out the metal bowls and spoons for dinner. The contents in the big red enameled pot only had a few minutes left to cook. As they waited, everyone but Mackay settled into contented silence, enjoying being around each other, though Lili's little stomach kept interrupting the quiet with gurglings and grumblings of protest. The scents of sweet cornbread baking and spicy peppers and tomatoes cooking filled the girls' nostrils. It caused their taste buds to water as Patty's chili simmered in the pot and Carey's bread finished in the cast iron skillet resting in the hot coals. Then nagging thoughts began to creep into their minds, spoiling the moment. Aphina. The ghost of her presence seemed to dampen their hunger, but she could not be avoided. They discussed a few ideas about where they could scout for her with the daylight that remained. After making one or two decisions, the girls watched the squirrels chattering and fighting over fallen nuts until their mom called out, "Supper's ready!"

While Lili tried to dish hot chili into a small cup to serve as a fairy plate, Mackay rubbed her hands together greedily. Saying grace was a bit awkward because of Mackay, but Carey only had to flick her tiny hand once. She had tried to steal cornbread when she thought everyone's eyes were closed.

"This sure smells good," Mackay said. "At least you people in Mitch-i-gun make good food."

Mackay was eating with a tiny wooden spoon. Ella had whittled it out of a small twig after they had finished her fairy house.

"Hope you like it," Patty said, as everyone started eating.

"Can I have some more?" Carey held out her bowl before the other girls had eaten half of their servings.

Ella raised an eyebrow at her older sister.

"What? I'm hungry," Carey said defensively.

As Carey grabbed her refilled bowl, a few nearby chickadees began to sing their tell-tale song.

"Chicka-dee-dee, chicka-dee-dee."

Then two fat little birds glided down from a lower limb to eat a few crumbs that had fallen from Lili's corn bread.

"They must eat a lot of camp scraps, 'cause the birds around here are really fat," Lili said, throwing out some more crumbs. Fluttering a few feet away, the two chickadees shied back. They stood there watching as if to assess the danger, but soon enough the breadcrumbs enticed them. With little hops on their stubby black legs, they jumped closer. Like little gentlemen in gray coats, with white vests, they jigged back and forth and left to right. Their dance brought them closer and closer to the food they wanted. Everyone watched this merry little performance and smiled as the birds ate all the breadcrumbs. Lili gave them some more.

Little by little one of the chickadees came within a few inches of Lili's open palm, and everyone held their breath, watching it peck the ground with its tiny black beak. Lili's eyes twinkled, and she gasped with excitement. The scene captured everyone's attention—except, that is, for a third chickadee who chose that very moment to land near the four open water bottles. As it sat on its perch above the bottles, it poked its head into each one, as far as it could without getting stuck. It was quick and efficient, like a mother bird putting food into a baby bird's mouth. Before anyone could notice the new bird, it darted off. The only clue to its departure was the slight brushing of its wings against the steel bottles as it thrust into flight. Once the new bird was safely seated on a nearby branch, it fluttered its wings like a signal flag, and the first two chickadees spooked and flew way. The first bird had nearly touched Lili's outstretched hand.

"Aww, so close," Lili said with a frustrated shrug of her shoulders as she returned to her seat on the log.

"Mackay, eat up! We have a lot of looking around to do after supper," Ella said as she handed Carey an open water bottle.

"Chili smells better than it tastes," Mackay protested, sticking out her tongue in disgust, "besides, I need to find some special flowers and leaves before dark. I want to make a pair of hiking boots for our adventure tomorrow."

Lili pinched one wing gently as if she was holding onto a dragonfly and said, "Drink a little water and finish your supper first, then you can go." Before Mackay could protest, Lili held up her bottle and offered the fairy a long cool drink. "You know," she added, as Mackay wiped her mouth with her sleeve, "you wear a lot of shoes for someone that doesn't do a lot of walking!"

Mackay stuck out her tongue and crossed her eyes at Lili, before she wolfed down her dinner. They all chuckled as she exaggeratedly gagged and swallowed the last few bites. After scraping the bowl clean, she held it out for all to see. She waited with an impatient expression, enduring the moments it took for them all to confirm that she had indeed eaten all her supper. Right before Patty gave her consent, Mackay tensed, like a runner waiting for the shot from the starting pistol, but then Patty nodded that she could go. Like a yellow comet of fairy fire, she shot across the clearing, down the trail, and out into the meadow nearby.

"You had better go and keep her out of trouble," suggested Patty, looking at Lili.

"Sure thing, Mom," Lili answered as she took one last gulp from her water bottle. Wiping her mouth and hands off on a napkin, she set her dinner bowl on the nearest rock, and ran off after Mackay.

"Don't skip out on all the dishes," Ella said to her sister with a broad, good-natured grin.

"And don't be gone too long. We have to go scouting around before it gets too dark," Patty said to Lili as she ran towards the clearing. They watched her go and finished up their meal. Soon enough it would be time to clean up the dishes, but a few moments without distractions seemed a good time to discuss where to start their search.

As they talked, Lili followed Mackay's trail of sparks out into the open meadow. The thigh-high grasses waved in the warm summer breeze as she cut a path right through the center of the glen. Everywhere she looked were patches of daises and dandelions, and sprinkled over it all were touches of some types of red and blue wildflowers. She did not know their names, but the red ones were like little cups with their insides painted yellow, and the blue ones had delicate petals that jetted out on all sides like little tutus dancing in the breeze. In the middle of the field she found Mackay, sitting on a white frilled cushion of Queen Anne's lace, just watching the grasses blow in the wind. Joining her, Lili sat down. The spot was a knoll that rushed up like an island in the midst of the sea of grass.

"Whatcha doing?" Lili asked.

"Nothing much. Just watching. I like watching," answered Mackay. "What are you doing?"

"Just looking for you, but now that I've found you, I'm going to lie right here for a few minutes and enjoy the clouds. How's that sound?" Lili asked, as she lay down and linked her hands behind her head.

Lili stretched out in the luxurious grass and breathed deeply. The warm evening air filled her nose with the fresh scents of rich earth, sun-toasted grass, and sweet flowers. She closed her eyes and filled her lungs with as many of these scents as she could hold, before she opened her eyes again and looked into the clear blue sky. Lili was one of those children privileged to have learned to enjoy simply doing nothing. She had learned how to be quiet long enough that a place could seep into her soul. So she lay there and ran her fingers through the blades of grass and plucked dandelions. Then she blew on their puffy white heads and watched the white strands float away as the clouds rolled by.

Mackay flittered off her flower throne and lay down beside Lili. Her new lounging spot was on a small rock embedded in the ground near her friend. With her legs crossed and her hands folded behind her head, she totally forgot about finding the flowers and grasses needed for her new shoes, in perfect fairy fashion. After a few moments she stretched out her arms to their furthest extent. Then, almost swallowing her fist with a yawn, she mumbled, "That cloud looks like a dragon."

"Yeah, and that one looks like a pig with stumpy legs. See it? That wispy one looks like its curly tail," Lili said, pointing at an especially fat and round cloud that did indeed look like a stumpy pig.

"That one reminds me of the fairy trees in our hollow back home," Mackay whispered, as her head nodded and her eyes drooped.

"And that one..." Lili trailed off with a big yawn. Her tired eyes blinked repeatedly before they closed. Within moments they were both sound asleep.

CHAPTER 10

Waking Up

PITCH BLACK DARKNESS. FUZZY THOUGHTS. A small line of light piercing the midst of endless bleakness. Then finally, blurry images dancing on the surface of what looked like cloudy water. These were the first glimpses of consciousness that stirred Lili as she awoke sometime later. She felt like an exhausted child shaken awake on the first day of school. The very last thing she wanted was to get up. Eyes wide open, she looked like an owl disturbed from its daytime nap. She blinked repeatedly, but nothing seemed to help to clear away the sleepiness from her eyes.

"I must've fallen asleep," she slurred as she fought against the drowsiness. "Mackay, we'd better get back to camp before they wonder where we've been all this time," Lili added as the fog in her mind cleared and her eyes started to focus again.

She noticed that Mackay was still asleep. Her little figure was posed like a picture in a story book. Her childlike face was framed by her curls, her hands were tucked under her cheek like a pillow, and her fairy fire burned with a dim yellowish glow around her head. As Lili looked at the sleeping fairy, she thought she almost appeared innocent.

"Mackay, come on! You can't sleep now. Mom's probably wondering where we are," said Lili, but the only response was a tiny little snore as the fairy rolled over.

"Come on, sleepy head! Time to get up," Lili coaxed. As she spoke, she crawled over to the fairy and nudged her with a finger, like she was poking a roly-poly bug. When Mackay did not respond, Lili gently picked her up. She was starting to feel a little concerned, but how does a person shake a fairy awake without hurting her? She just sat there holding her, and was about to call out her name again, when she was struck with an idea.

"Hey, enough playing around," Lili laughed, and then blew on her face ever so gently. She hoped it was just a fairy prank, but Mackay would not wake up. No matter what Lili did, she

Waking Up

lay there, limp in her hand, her arms and legs drooping over the edge like wilted flowers over the edge of a pot.

Fear stabbed at Lili's heart as she cupped the delicate little form in her hands and ran back to camp.

"Mom, Mom, something's wrong with Mackay!" Lili yelled, bursting through the underbrush.

She came to a skidding halt beside one of the logs. Her breath caught in her throat as she looked around. The scene turned her legs to water, caused her shoulders to stoop, and her arms to go limp. *What had happened?* she thought. The chili pot and corn bread pan had been knocked from their perch on one of the large stones. The remaining food had been spilled on the ground, splattered all over their white tablecloth, and splashed all over the nearest log. The crumbs of bread were strewn about as if a madman had been feasting on it. Carey and Ella were slumped over, their bodies lying very still on the logs they had been sitting on. The bowls and spoons were scattered haphazardly around the camp. Each one had been licked clean by eager tongues. She noticed chili- covered paw prints all around the camp. They started by the food, seemed to gather around her sisters and then cross to where... Her stomach clenched as a question formed in her mind: *Where's Mom?*

Lili scanned the camp again, more carefully this time,

refusing to believe what her senses were telling her. Carefully she placed Mackay on her sleeping bag and inched over to Carey and Ella. She hoped being closer to them might bring her a little comfort. "Mom," Lili called out, like a child awakened from a bad dream. Then, with growing force she cried out, her voice high-pitched and tight with panic, as mounting concern added strength to her words, "Mom, where are you?"

Her throat constricted with fear, which is what happens, my reader, when you realize you are really and truly alone. With determination she pushed away the terror that threatened her mind. Her heart began to beat rapidly, and her palms began to sweat as she traced the animal tracks one more time. They all led to the space where she had last seen her mother sitting. It looked as if something or someone had been dragged off.

With anger, fear, and frustration she cried out, "Mom!" She followed the trail a few feet into the woods and then thought better of it. She ran back to her older sisters and tried to wake them. Falling to the ground beside them, she patted their faces and called their names. "Carey. Come on, Carey! Wake up!" she cried with choking sobs, but Carey would not stir. She looked over to Ella. "Come on, Ella, wake up," she moaned as tears rolled down her cheeks. Suddenly the undeniable facts crushed in on her little heart, and her knees buckled. Lili sat there for a few moments holding her eldest sister's hand. She clutched Carey's palm and rubbed it with her fingers like a superstitious man rubs a lucky rabbit's foot. The gears of her mind were jammed, and she struggled to think clearly. Minutes passed as spasms of sorrow rocked her body. Each time she thought of her mother, her chest became tight and her heart felt pinched. Every contraction forced out streams of tears and wailing sobs. Seeking comfort, she clutched her knees to her chest and cried.

As she rocked herself and deep despair threatened to overwhelm her, a dim light pierced the darkness. It was like a warm cheery window shining out into a dark stormy night. She had been lost, but now it called to her and gave her a hope of finding her way back home. Her heart ached, but through the howling winds of doubt she heard her mother's voice whisper, "Think truth." Her emotions rebelled, but she clenched her fists in defiance and willed the darkness away. *Truth*, she thought. The dark feelings made it hard to find, but finally she glimpsed it. She forced herself to remember the truths her parents had sprinkled into the soft soil of her heart since her childhood. She fought. She grasped at them and clutched them. In desperation her mind found purchase and gripped with all its might to these little roots. With determination she focused her thoughts and truth lifted her out of the ditch she had fallen into.

Rubbing the tears from her cheeks, she tried to stand. Now that truth had a firm hold on her, she spoke with growing confidence to herself, "Okay Lili, you have a job to do. You're the only one awake around here, so you'll have to be the one that decides the next thing to do." Talking to herself helped. It had a way of pushing back the loneliness.

Then she remembered something. "Well, Dad always says, 'You can't know the way to get where you're going until you know the place you're starting from,' so I guess I need to figure out where I'm at."

Taking a deep breath, Lili started by listing the facts as she saw them: "Mom's gone, and I can't go off and get her all alone." As she said these words out loud, stated so matter-of-factly, they threatened her weak resolve. *I will have to think about that later*, Lili thought. Before she could bog down in a quagmire of emotions, she jumped ahead to the next thing she knew: "Carey and Ella are still here, and I think they are just sleeping." To assure herself of that fact, she bent over and placed her ear beside their gaping mouths. After checking for breathing and smelling their chili-scented breaths, she felt more reassured. Then she added to herself, "If I woke up, they should

Waking Up

wake up too." When she realized this truth and it settled into her heart, hope—real tangible hope—stood up and cheered her tremendously. It was like looking behind a taunting bully and seeing your big, strong, older brother coming to the rescue.

After she had turned these thoughts over in her mind, she decided it was best to try and wake up her sisters again. Thinking over her options, she finally said to herself, "Maybe water will help." She grabbed the only bottle that still had water in it and tipped it over. With a little bit of naughty delight, she poured the water right on Carey's face. It soaked her sister, but it did not wake her up. As she sat there looking at the water streaming over Carey's face, she noticed something. The water had a strange tint to it, and there were tiny bits and flecks mixed into it. "What's this?" Lili asked, bending over to take a closer look.

Puzzled, Lili's mind turned the problem around and around, looking at it from every angle. Her mind flashed to the fat birds and remembered their strange behavior. Suddenly everything clicked into place. "Aphina."

Speaking that name sent a blast of wintry air down her spine. With tenacity she clung to the truth like a child holding onto a parent's coattails when learning to ice skate. She comforted herself with the fact that at least she had figured out *how*

Aphina had managed to steal away her mother. Dear reader, sometimes, in the hardest moments, it is the little battles that mean the most.

"Well, if I'm right, Aphina drugged me. But... I woke up. Since I woke up without help, that must mean that sooner or later Carey and Ella will wake up too. Maybe I will just have to wait." She looked around. "Mom always says, 'A watched pot never boils.' So, I guess the best thing to do is try to clean up and make sure everything's ready when they do wake up."

With her decision made, there was nothing else to do but to do it. The first thing she did was stoke the fire. Using a long stick, she stirred up the coals and added an armful of dry wood. A roaring fire would help. The last thing she wanted was to be alone *and* in the dark. The next thing to do was to make everyone comfortable. She did her best to pull her two big sisters off the logs. It was difficult, but she managed to flop them at least half-way onto their sleeping bags. Then she got out her knife, followed by Carey's. Since Ella was lying on her side, she figured her knife was too much work to fish out. If she did need a knife, she figured she could only use two anyway. To be prepared, she opened the sharp Swiss army knives her father had bought them a few summers back and placed them on a nearby log. That way they would be ready if she needed them.

It's better to be safe than sorry, she thought. She used a pine branch to sweep up the mess, then she washed the dishes. After putting everything away, Lili said to herself, "Maybe later I can make a spear out of a stick, but I'm definitely not going into the woods by myself!" There was nothing much left to do now.

It would be very dark soon. "Please, let them wake up before it gets too dark," Lili breathed a prayer.

"Now what?" she said looking around. Idleness had cleared a spot in her mind, and fear was trying to fill the void. Just as fear crept back, she was distracted by Mackay. She was rolling on the sleeping bag, as if she was rousing from a terrible dream. Her sisters were still sound asleep, but Mackay seemed to be stirring. Lili decided to give it a try. Maybe this time she would be able to wake her up, but to her great disappointment, no amount of tapping, shaking, or talking could wake her. Mackay seemed locked in a shallow, restless dream.

After a few more uncomfortable minutes sitting on the log and looking around for something to do, Lili picked up Ella's bag. She never thought she would have any extra time for reading when she packed her bags. There was Aphina's book, though. The thought of its magic made her a little nervous, but she could not think of anything else to do. When she opened the middle zipper and pulled out the old leather book, a laminated picture fell out. Ella must have been using it as a bookmark. Lili laid the large book on her lap and bent down to pick the photo up. Then she saw who it was—Mom. Her mother was laughing and hugging her smiling father. Her happy mouth was surrounded by smile lines, her blonde eyebrows were raised in happy arches, her blue eyes were soft and warm. One teardrop escaped from the corner of Lili's eye. She did not have too many left. She caressed the photo with a finger and made a vow, "Mom, we'll find you, I promise." As she spoke, her voice was firm with determination. She placed the picture into the bag and opened the book.

"Let's see what we can find to pass the time, shall we? But Lili, remember, no bad guys," she spoke aloud, as she started fumbling through the first few stories. "The Soldier and the Tree Sprite, ooh, that sounds good," Lili said to herself, after scanning the illustrated pages to check for bad guys.

Lili started reading and the words seemed to restrain her loneliness. They filled up the darkness like a cheery fire and warmed her heart. Books were so familiar, like opening a package from home while away at summer camp. Soon she was totally absorbed, and my dear reader, I am sure you would like this story too, for it was quite diverting. It was a story about a wandering soldier of fortune that became lost in a mystical forest. Just as Lili was reaching the part when the soldier meets the tree sprite, Mackay began to stir. She opened her eyes and her head wobbled as if she could not shake off her sleepiness. She stretched out like a cat waking up after a nap in the sun and yawned deeply.

"Mmm...aaah," Mackay said and scratched her head, "I must've been tired, I slept like Oberon."

"What?" Lili asked, laughing at the fairy as she scrunched her face and smiled sleepily.

"Oberon. Don't you humans know anything?" asked Mackay in a terse, irritated manner. "He was the Fairy king that had a spell cast on him so that he slept so long his beard grew and grew and covered his entire body. You must've heard of it. My mother told me that story every night before I went to bed. It's one of my favorites." She added these last points with mounting disbelief at the blank look on Lili's face.

"Never heard of it," Lili said with a shrug. She had her finger resting on the open page to mark her spot, while she patiently waited to get back to her story. "You did sleep a long time though."

"Must be the food that you eat here that makes you sleep so long. Look at Carey and Ella, they're still sleeping and it's not even bedtime," Mackay said, pointing at the girls that were snoring ever so slightly.

"Well, it's something like that. We'll have to wait for them to wake up," Lili said, but shivered a bit at the thought of going to bed alone. The lengthening shadows seemed to be stretching out to grab her. It was her grasp on the truth alone that pushed back her fears. Resolutely she decided she was not going to deal with nighttime until she had to.

"Where's your mother?" Mackay asked as she flew over to Lili's shoulder and flitted around her head. "Have you been crying? Why's there dirt on your face? There's something wrong, isn't there?" Mackay asked the questions in clipped succession, touching the rounded cheek of the eight-year old's face.

Lili's eyes looked like disturbed pools for a brief moment before she managed to answer, "Aphina took her." She said this quietly, willing herself to be strong, each word growing in volume. Each word took effort. "The water made us sleep. My mom was gone when I woke up. Aphina took her. Carey and Ella are still sleeping, because they must've drunk more than we did."

Mackay's response was stoic. Her wings barely moved, fanning rhythmically, like a butterfly perched on a flower. Lili saw what must have been a torrent of memories pass before those miniature hazel eyes. The beautiful child-like face grew pensive and muted, a funny-looking expression for a fairy. The fairy fire that had moments before been a faint purple began to burn bright, crimson red.

"She took my mother, too," Mackay said, looking at Lili with compassion.

"Mackay, I'm sorry," Lili offered, "I—I didn't know."

"That's not your fault. I didn't tell you. It was one of those things that I said I'd rather not talk about. It was a long time ago, right before Aphina allowed the Fairy folk to be sold into slavery. But there is nothing that can be done now. She's with the Lord of Songs in the Waking Lands and she's *never* coming back," said Mackay, wiping hot tears from her eyes. Then she stood up in defiance, stretching to all of her three inches of height. "I couldn't do anything then, but I *shall* do something now."

"Thanks, Mackay," Lili said, kissing the top of the little curly head. "I'm sure when the time comes, you will. But right now, we just have to wait for my sisters to wake up. I figure there is nothing better to do but be patient and keep the fire going. I could really use some company, though. Want to read the book with me?" she asked. Mackay started smiling again and sat down on Lili's knee, the one not covered by the book.

"I can't read your language," Mackay explained.

"Well, this story seems safe enough, how about I read it to you?"

"Would you really?" asked Mackay.

"Yeah, Mom always says there's nothing like a good book on a bad day," Lili said with a smile. "I was at a really good part where the soldier meets a tree sprite. See the picture?" Lili pointed at the illustration.

"I love tree sprites. They are so kind and wise. Back home in the great forests of the Kingdom of Frey they tried to help us. They were our allies when we tried to escape Aphina's slave traders. When the soldiers destroyed our homes in the great castle, they hid as many of us as they could in the forest." Mackay looked at the picture with interest.

"The story is a little harder than I am used to. Mom normally reads the hard ones to me." Mackay looked a bit skeptical, so Lili quickly added, "But my Nana says I'm a good reader for my age." With a nod from Mackay, Lili eagerly began the story, "*Perin was ex...haust...ed,*" Lili read, sounding out the hard word. "*How had he become lost in this Light-for...sak...en forest anyway? The Wise Ones say the pattern weaves as it wills, but he fi...gured it was playing tricks on him today.*

"*Finally he sat beside a rowan tree to rest. The stones in his boots were un..bear..able. They had been bo..ther..ing* him ever since he had passed through the old a...band...on...ed quarry. As he pulled off his left boot, he counted four small stones. They tumbled out one after the other. 'How do they get in there?' he asked himself as he rubbed his short red beard. It always itched when he let it grow in.

"After replacing his boots, he leaned back to clear his head. Why am I here anyway? he thought. Fire swamps, dwarves, talking animals, what next? For what reason has the Light sent me here?

"Perin reached into his bag and grabbed his flute. The feel of the in..stru...ment in his hands gave him great comfort. There was something so right about holding it and playing it. Without thinking, his fingers started to play a tune. His ten...sion melted away as his fingers un...con..scious...ly," Lili fumbled through the word, "skipped about to play 'The Black Nag,' a lively jig from the river country.

"The notes danced on the breeze. The trees seemed to stir with the happy, tril...ling music. Perin lost himself in the music. All he knew was the song, and the song filled his mind with pictures of home and feast days. He was so ab...absorb...ed he was unaware of the effect of his music around him.

"The cre...vices and folds in the rowan tree's bark became the gar-ments covering an en...chant...ing, robed woman," Lili sounded out. "The sprite within the tree awoke, re...spond...ing to his joy...ous music. With each passing note, she became more of a woman, and less a tree. Her flowing locks of long brown hair were filled with beautiful leaves a...adorn...ing it like yellow flowers..."

Even with a few pauses to sound out difficult words, Lili and Mackay were lost in their story. This is why they did not notice the lone yellow leaf, the one which blew out from between the pages as she turned it to read the next. The yellow leaf had serrated edges, and it was burnished with a flaming red tip. Like a kite with a broken string, it was carried away from the book by a gust of air. It spun, twirling down and landing right behind them on the ground. As Lili and Mackay read, their imaginations assumed the music they heard was make-believe, just the product of a story that felt so real that hearing music would only be natural. And the smells of the magical forest blended so well with the scents of the actual forest around them, that they did not notice the aromas wafting from the pages of the book.

The leaf itself landed and rocked on the last breath of air before lying completely still in the short grass. Within moments the stem grew. It stretched, piercing into the soil as it descended into the dirt like a worm wiggling underground.

Then the leaf split, growing into the base of a small tree. Roots grew, rising and falling through the soil. While the roots spread, the branches of the tree stretched to the heavens. They were growing unfettered by the normal workings of time. They expanded and spread like a peacock's tail, all splendid, green and glorious. Moments later, each little twig sprouted buds and the buds blossomed into flowers, then these shed their petals, dusting the ground with a shower of delicate white raindrops. Petal by spinning petal they dropped, and the grass was slowly carpeted around the base of the tree. It covered it like a white veil about the feet of a blushing bride. The flowers yielded their places to clusters of ripe red berries. In these few, but magical moments, the changes came unnoticed by the pair. Unnoticed, that is, until a long willowy hand reached out and touched Lili ever so gently upon her shoulder.

Lili jumped. Her startled scream sent an explosion of fearful blue fire bursting out of Mackay. Lili was too afraid to turn around and could only whisper, "Please, please don't be Aphina." Taking a deep breath, she forced herself to look behind her. What she saw was a smiling face. She did not have to wonder who this sprite was. She was, after all, exactly like the illustration in the book. Lili first noticed her soft tender eyes. They reminded her of her Granny's eyes, and that had the instant effect of calming her fears.

Now that she felt more certain, she spoke. "Hello. I'm sorry I screamed. You sure did startle me." She and Mackay both gave little curtsies before they introduced themselves. Now reader, this might seem a strange thing for them to do, but a person does not meet royalty every day. This tree sprite had an air about her. As they stood before her, they felt as if they were being inspected by a queen—a benevolent queen—but a queen, nonetheless. The sprite returned their curtsies with a little bow of her own, after which Lili added, "My name is Lili, and this is Mackay."

"I see that I startled you, child of the woods, but you have no need to be afraid. I am a tree sprite. My name is Hetre, in the language of your people. And as for the Fairy folk, I know them well," the sprite said. The soft sound of her voice was like wind passing through the treetops in early summer, "I greet you Fairy child, may your fire always burn brightly," she said with a formal bow of her head.

"And I greet you, Spirit of the Tree. May your roots always find water," Mackay responded with a deep, graceful bow. If Mackay's response was any indication, this woman was of some importance, because Lili had never seen her act this seriously before. Lili did notice, though, that Mackay's eyes still sparkled with mischief.

"Now child, may I ask you what has brought me here to this place where the trees sleep so soundly?"

"My lady," said Lili, adding the title that only seemed proper when speaking to her, "I was reading with my friend when you came out of our story book. There really wasn't anything else to do while we waited for my sisters to wake up."

"Well then, the Father of all Trees indeed must have sent me here. 'Grow where you are planted.' That *is* what the ancient oaks say." Her words were smooth, and her limbs seemed to dance more than move. Lili knew with each passing moment, that this tree sprite could be trusted. She did not know why she knew this, but a deep confidence settled in her mind. Maybe the assurance came from her peaceful face, and her manner of speaking to her. It really did remind her of all the things she loved about being with her Granny. Granny always took her seriously and spoke to her like an adult. She was very wise in that way. Then Hetre patted the log laying before her, and said, "Please, sit down, child. There is no need to remain standing."

Lili sat back down, but Mackay chose to hover next to Lili's shoulder. Speaking to the fairy, Lili said, "This is amazing! Wait till I tell Carey and Ella all about this. They'll be sooo jealous when they wake up!"

"Are Carey and Ella the two maidens that lie nearby, child?" Hetre asked.

"Yes, my lady," Lili answered.

"They sleep very deeply, I see, and you speak as if you cannot wake them. Has something befallen them? Some type of enchantment?" asked the kind tree sprite. Her words held such concern that they forever dispelled any doubts that lurked in the back of Lili's mind about her new friend.

"Yes, my lady. An evil witch has also escaped from our reading book. She's really bad. She's the one that put some kinda potion in our water. No matter what I do, I can't wake 'em up. I was just waiting, hoping they would wake up by themselves. I didn't really know what else to do."

CHAPTER 11

Help

"INTRIGUING," SAID HETRE. "MY CHILD, IT seems the Father of all Trees *has* sent me here after all. Being born of the tree-folk, we the sprites know all the wisdom to be found in plants and herbs. We know their uses for healing and fixing of ailments of almost all that suffer," said Hetre. She did not say this as a boast, but as a simple statement of the facts.

"Small sister," Hetre said, addressing Mackay now, "It appears as if this world's soil binds me. It is unlike the soil of my home. My feet here are deeply rooted, and they still sleep. Therefore, I will need your help. I know your people learn the plants of the woods. If I tell you the names of the things that I will need, would you be so kind as to gather them for me?"

"Yes, Tree Sprite, I can do that for you. But I must confess that I've found Mitch-i-gun to be a strange land. I just hope that I'll find what you need."

"Since the Tree Father has brought me here, I am certain he will provide what is necessary. 'He always tills the ground before he plants.' Come closer, small sister," the sprite commanded, and Mackay obeyed. She flew near to hear the whispered words. The sprite gave the instructions, counting off each item on her long fingers as Mackay's head bobbed up and down as she listened.

"Yes, I know of that one," she said in response to a question, then "Yes, that one too," and then finally she said in amazement, "Oh, that can do that? I never knew!"

Hetre finished by saying, "That should be all." Mackay's reply was to smile and bow. Then she turned and shot off, followed by a yellow blur of fairy fire.

"She will not be long, I hope. The Fairy folk are wonderful companions, but their youthfulness makes them prone to distraction," explained the sprite. She folded her arms across her chest with a contented smile and waited for the fairy's return. She looked like a proud mother anticipating her child's return home from her first day of school. Her eyes were hopeful yet mixed with a little bit of anxiety.

Lili also realized she could do nothing but wait, so she did. She made herself comfortable and chatted with the sprite. As she talked with Hetre about her home, she kicked her feet back and forth, and from time to time she tapped the tips of her shoes together.

After probably a few more minutes than it should have taken, Mackay zipped between them and interrupted their conversation. Perched on her shoulder were a few wildflowers: one white and one bluish purple, and in her other hand were two herbs and a small piece of some bark. "Here, I found them," said Mackay, dropping her burdens with a grunt onto a large stone close to Hetre. The load must have been heavy for her, because she wiped her forehead and gave a sigh of relief before she added, "The last herb you named was a bit of a challenge, but I found it anyway," her words coming between labored breaths.

"Well, small sister, you have honored your people," Hetre said as Mackay puffed out her chest with pride and her fire burned a radiant orange. "Child of the woods, I will need your help. Could you please take the things our sister has brought, and bring with them a bowl and some stones?"

"Yes, my lady," Lili replied.

"You will need to follow my instructions closely, my child. Are you ready?" she asked Lili.

Lili gave a confident nod of her head and dropped a quick curtsy. She turned and grabbed two metal bowls, a few large flat stones, and a knife and spoon, just in case she might need them.

When all was laid out before them on the stone Hetre began with the instructions. "Start with the bark, my dear. Take a stone and carefully grind it into powder if you can. If you use the large stone as your table and the small rock as a grinder, it should make the job easier. If you cannot grind it into powder, do not fret yourself. It is hard to do so on your first try. As long as you can turn it into small pieces, it will still have the desired effect. After that you will need to place the powder into one of the bowls. Then, my child, you will lay the two herbs with the powder. You will add a few drops of water and use the stone again to smash all of it into a paste. Is that clear, my child?"

Lili nodded her head and repeated them back to Hetre, just to make sure she had not forgotten anything. Then she started. After a few minutes and a smashed finger, Lili was beginning to figure things out and was smiling broadly at her progress. Hetre gave her words of encouragement and bits of instruction now and then when she felt she needed it, but she did quite well for her first time.

"Now child, we will use the fire," Hetre explained. "Please place some clean water in a pot. You will need about four cups full. Once the water is boiling you will add the paste and the flowers, my dear. When the water becomes quite dark in color, you will pour the tea carefully into two cups." Lili quickly obeyed, gathering the necessary things and placing the water on the rack over the fire so that it would boil. Once it was mixed and cooking Hetre added, "My child, I almost forgot, you will need to use something to strain the flowers and larger pieces to keep them from going into the tea cups."

"She can use this cloth, Tree Sprite," interrupted Mackay as she offered her a handkerchief. She had borrowed it from Carey's bag.

"Yes, Fairy child, that will do nicely," Hetre said. Her words were not hard, but their edges were stiff and formal, a subtle rebuke. Mackay *had* forgotten her manners and interrupted.

An odd sort of tea was soon brewing in the pot. Lili was trying hard to 'not watch.' It was all quite uncomfortable, and took a bit of effort. When someone is trying their hardest not to peek, that is when it seems the hardest not to do so. It made her want to fidget, but Hetre smiled at her and encouraged her to wait patiently. Being a tree, she had acquired this important skill—the discipline of being still. With a little effort Lili found her patience rewarded. It was like waiting for one's birthday and then waking up to find the day had finally come. Soon it was bubbling, and little wisps of steam were snaking out the spout. She was surprised how strong the scent was that filled her nose. The floral smell reminded Lili a little of her father's favorite tea, Earl Grey. It had that same perfumey, grassy scent about it. Inspecting it, Lili wondered if it would taste good or not. She was somehow certain it would taste like some of the herbal medicines her mother made them take at times. If so, she was glad it was theirs and not hers. With her shaking hands covered in hot mitts, she poured the steaming brew through the handkerchief into two metal camping cups. She did her best not to spill any.

"Now my child, wait until the tea is cool, and then help your siblings to drink it slowly. Do not spill. I do not know how powerful the magic is that causes your sisters to slumber. We may need all of it if we are to wake them," said Hetre with a soft touch of her hand on Lili's cheek. Lili noticed that the skin of her hand was smooth. It was not rough like one would think a tree would be. It felt like a smoothed piece of wood covered with fine sawdust before the carpenter wipes it—delicate, soft, and comforting.

Once the drinks had cooled a little, Lili held the first cup by the brim and tiptoed carefully over to Carey. She set the warm cup down on a log, and propped Carey up as best she could. Carey's head slumped. Every time Lili raised Carey's chin, she mumbled and clenched her teeth. The last thing Lili wanted was to get bitten while she tried to open Carey's mouth.

"Come on, Carey, open up," Lili coaxed. She sounded like she was talking to one of her baby dolls back at home. "Time for your medicine," Lili said while tipping her head back and holding her mouth open with two fingers.

"You look like you're enjoying this," Mackay said, "even if you're trying to hide it."

"The shoe's on the other foot now. I'm always the one having to take it. I've never been the one to give it out before," Lili said as she dripped a small amount of tea in Carey's open mouth.

"Slowly, my child," reminded the Sprite. Her voice was firm but calm. It reminded Lili to stop being so playful. What she was doing was important.

"Please work," Lili whispered.

At first, Carey coughed a little as the tea filled her mouth, but before it dribbled out, she started to swallow small amounts of the stuff. Lili felt a little like Heather, a character in one of her favorite stories. She had always wondered what it would be like to be a nurse. As the concoction began to work, Carey began sipping the tea as if she were in a dreamy tea-party. When she finished half the cup, Lili stopped. That was when Carey gave a jaw-popping yawn and fought to open her sleepy eyes.

"What," Carey pressed her lips together and frowned, "what is that?" she slurred, looking down at the cup in disgust.

Lili put down the cup and hugged her sister's neck, "You're awake!"

"Wow, I feel like trash," Carey said, "what happened?" She sounded like she had cotton balls stuffed in her mouth, then she touched her head and rubbed her temples as if she had a headache. After a moment or two she finally sat up, but she swayed back and forth ever so slightly, like a person who is dizzy from spinning around too much.

"Finish your tea," Lili commanded. Her voice was stern, but Mackay could tell from the twinkle in her eyes that she was enjoying being the boss for a change. "And I'll wake up Ella. *Then* I'll explain everything."

It was not too long before Carey and Ella were both awake and sitting up, though neither of them were wide-eyed, let alone happy about how they felt. Lili sat opposite them and in front of the tree sprite. They should have wondered who or what she was, but both of them were still too fuzzyheaded to be certain of anything. As they listened, Lili told them what she knew about the last hour or two, and Mackay did her part by interrupting. She wanted to make sure to fill in the details she thought Lili had left out.

When all the story was told, the girl's minds rocked, floundering in the waves of confusion, sorrow, and sleepiness. It was all too much at first. After some moments of silence, Carey's numb mind found its way to some solid footing. Now that she was grounded, she felt she had to make a decision. She could not and would not give up. Her sisters needed her.

As for Ella, all the difficult circumstances and the sudden loss of her mother had weakened her firm grip on her feelings. The news had toppled her composure. The raging river of her emotions, normally so controlled and channeled, had run over its banks. The resulting flood had swept away her resolve. Not sure what else to do, she turned, covered her face with her hands, and started to cry. Streams of tears ran down her cheeks and her shoulders began to shake. She knew all too well that their eyes were watching her, and she burned with embarrassment. She could feel her face flush and redden. It was too much, so she ran to the edge of the forest where she felt she might hide her shame in the mingling of the firelight and the twilight of the woods. As she fled, Hetre and Lili reached out sympathetic hands. They had a deep desire to comfort her, but Carey stilled them. She also pinched Mackay's wings together,

as you do when you are catching a butterfly, and told her to stay put. Mackay crossed her arms and frowned as her whole body crackled red with annoyed fairy fire, but she obeyed. "I'll go," Carey said.

Carey walked slowly over. When she was close enough, she placed a hand on her sister's shoulder. The shoulder was trembling. "Come here," Carey said in a whisper, as she opened her arms to her sister. Ella turned and hid her face in her sister's embrace. They stood there for some time, no one speaking, until Ella had cried it all out. The tears were followed by full blown anger. The more she thought about the circumstances, the madder she got. She hated to feel out of control. She did not want to be weak.

The anger in her heart and mind could not be contained, it needed someplace to go, so it came out in one desperate question. With a shaking voice she asked, "Why, Carey?"

Carey waited, hoping some words of wisdom would come out of nowhere and tell her what to say. The seconds ticked by, and her sister looked at her expectantly. She felt the maturing weight of responsibility pressing on her shoulders. *What am I supposed to say?* she wondered. Just as she was about to say the typical 'it will all be fine' line and try somehow to encourage her sister, she remembered something.

"Ella, remember when we had that crazy month last year? Dad's bank lost his big money transfer from that company he had worked for overseas? Nobody had any idea where his paycheck was. It was just gone. Remember that while they tried to figure it all out, everything got really tight for Mom and Dad?" she asked.

"Yeah," Ella said, quite confused. Her furrowed brow and raised eyebrows seemed to say, *But what in the world does that have to do with anything, Carey?*

Carey pressed on, despite her sister's skepticism. "Remember how Dad kept calling the bank and asking what had happened to his money? He wanted to know why it was gone, and the bank just kept saying they were 'working on it.' We didn't hear anything for weeks. But what did Dad do?" Carey said with more confidence as each word led her to the next.

Ella seemed to stand up straighter, and she shook less as she listened. Carey hoped she had at least distracted her from her grief, when Ella answered her sister's question: "He finally decided to be patient. They couldn't give him any answers anyway, so he figured the only thing left to do was to get back to work."

"That's right. It was difficult for a while, but we finally got the money, and everything turned out in the end." Carey wiped away a stray tear on Ella's cheek as she added, "Ella, I don't know all the answers, but I think that if we get to work, and do what we can, that will go a long way in helping us to fix all this. Okay?"

Ella stood there silently, but Carey saw the truth sink in. Ella nodded in agreement, and Carey squeezed her in a tight hug. Then Ella hugged her back, which turned into a contest to see who could squeeze the hardest. Their laughter helped to chase away the remaining confusion and sadness. Ella had made her decision and her despair had been replaced by determination.

"Okay, Carey, let's try," Ella said with a broad smile.

Hand-in-hand they turned around and started back to the camp. Ella leaned in and whispered, "Thanks." In response Carey tried to give her a wink, but since she could never really manage a wink, it looked more like a funny, over-exaggerated blink.

As they returned, the awkward silence around the camp disappeared. Lili, Hetre, and Mackay were gathered around the campfire waiting to welcome them back.

Now that their minds were clear, Carey and Ella were shaken by the beauty of the tree sprite. The sprite was standing by their younger sister, and they noted every detail: the long slender limbs, the brown hair that flowed past her slim shoulders, each strand like individual grains of polished wood, her smooth, carved brow, her smile, sweet and pleasant like a warm spring breeze. Though moments before their hearts had been crammed to bursting with a passionate desire to make desperate plans, the sprite's still presence gave them pause. It begged for consideration, for time to think. The very air around her was heavy with the weight of wisdom.

"Children of the woods, I hope you have recovered from your fright?" asked Hetre with great concern. "Such news is distressing."

"Yes, my lady, we are fine," Carey replied.

"Carey and Ella, this is Hetre," Lili explained. "She came out of the book, but you probably guessed that. She helped me wake you up."

"Nice to meet you, Hetre," both girls said.

The tree sprite nodded her head in reply and reached out her long willowy fingers to shake their outstretched hands.

"I bet Hetre will be a great help when we look for Mom," Lili added. Her eyes shone with the light of hope as she grinned up into the face of the sprite.

"Oh, my child, I am afraid that the Father of all Trees has not sent me here for that purpose. Even now my roots dig deeper, and my limbs beckon me to sleep. I am not free to walk the woods with the children of men as I am in my homeland. It seems the Tree Father sees fit to send you ahead without me, child," Hetre said, cupping Lili's chin in her hands, as if holding a precious treasure.

"But you are no longer alone, child. Your brave older sisters are here to guide you, and together I am sure you will find your mother. Together you will rescue her. You, my child, have deep roots," Hetre said, touching the tip of Lili's nose with one of her outstretched fingers. "We sprites can see these things," she said with a smile and a nod of her head. "It is when the storm winds blow their hardest that the deeply rooted trees stand the firmest."

Lili almost cried at the sad news. She had not realized until that moment how deeply Hetre's presence had comforted her. Her chin quivered just a touch, but she managed a nod of her head.

She sat up straight and tall. "Yes, my lady. I'll miss you. Thank you for helping me... and for being a friend." Lili added, then she gave the sprite a tremendous hug.

"Yes, my child," said the sprite, returning Lili's embrace, "and thank you for calling me here to be a part of this wonderful adventure. Now before you children send me back to my home, I do wish to add a piece of advice. I think it might aid you in my absence."

"Yes, my lady, please do. Anything you can do is appreciated," said Ella.

"Remember this. We the trees grow slowly, and we live long years, but we do not sit idle. As the seasons pass, we watch the children of the woods and the children of men. My children, I tell you now what I have observed by watching evil men. Their wickedness batters them like the cold of approaching winter. It withers their souls, until, like an autumn leaf, the winds of their fears pluck them and carry them away. This is why they are more often running from something than they are going somewhere."

Once the counsel was given, the girls sat quietly. It was like they had been handed a half-finished Rubik's cube. They fiddled with this bit of wisdom, turning it around and around in their minds. After a few moments they still had not figured out what it had to do with their circumstances. They looked at one another. None of them were sure what to say until Carey answered for them all, "My lady, thank you for all you've done, and we'll try to remember your advice."

It was time to say goodbye. It was getting late, and the girls had lots of work to do before they could go to sleep. Each of the older girls stood in turn, shook the sprite's hand, and said her goodbye, but when it was Lili's turn, she ran to the sprite and embraced her. Her tight hug made the tree sprite groan. Once she caught her breath, she filled the air with a fond chuckle.

"It will be well child, you will see," she said in encouragement.

Lili backed away with a nod of her head, and Mackay drew closer to the sprite, as if she was approaching royalty. She bowed with a flutter of her wings. Her fairy light pulsed between red and yellow fire, the individual colors refusing to mix into any shade of orange. They simply flickered between the two. The girls sensed the pair needed privacy, so they looked in Zao's book to find the end of Hetre's story. After a few minutes of serious conversation, the pair parted with even more deep formal bows and flowery speeches. Though the girls missed most of it, and the words spoken were with such thick accents of Fairie and Sprite that the girls could barely understand their parting words, they caught a few things here and there. With one final bow, Mackay flew to Lili's side and sat down on her shoulder.

"I am ready, children. May the Father of all Trees guide you on your journey."

After Hetre's benediction Carey read the last sentence of her story. She took it slowly, like you do when you are savoring the last sunset on the last day of summer before school begins. As she read the words, *"The End,"* Hetre bowed her head, and her form faded away in ripples and waves like a mirage. As she disappeared, so did Lili's last hope that Hetre would change her mind and stay. One lone tear trickled down Lili's cheek as she waved a final goodbye.

With a sigh, the girls turned to look at each other and Carey closed the book.

"Now what?" Ella asked, looking around at the campsite. It seemed empty now that Hetre was gone.

"Well, for starters, let's get some more firewood. There's no use wandering around the woods all night. Maybe tomorrow we can try to follow the tracks the animals left behind. For now though, I think we all need a good night's sleep," Carey said as she set down the book and placed her knife back in her pocket.

"How much wood do we need, Carey?" Lili asked.

"As much as we can find close by. I want to make a couple extra fires around our camp. That should give us enough light, and keep any ani... uhh, yeah..." Carey cut off her words when she realized what she had almost told her little sister. Concerned, she looked at Lili as she tried to fix her mistake, "Yeah, I mean, that many fires will help to keep us warm all night." Carey noticed that Ella smirked at her, and her look said, *Way to go, sis! You almost put your foot in your mouth!*

"Okay, Carey," replied Lili, "I'll get my flashlight and the water bottles. We should probably fill them up at the tap by the boat dock," she said with a trusting smile.

"Good idea, Lili," Carey said, trying to sound reassuring. She patted her sister on the shoulder. She did not want to overdo it. She really wanted Lili to think they had everything under control.

As Lili got the bottles and found her flashlight, Carey pulled Ella aside. "Ella, you go with Lili, and stay on the path. Got it? Take the big flashlight with you and only pick up branches along the way, *not* in the woods. Don't be gone long, and make sure you two have your pocketknives with you. I'll take Mackay with me," Carey said.

"Gotcha. Come on Lili, let's go," Ella said. She tested the flashlight by clicking it off and on a few times to make sure it was working. The last thing she wanted was for the flashlight to go out on their way back to camp.

"I'm supposed to stay with Lili," Mackay pouted. "Hetre told me to watch over her. She made me promise," Mackay protested. Her hands were on her hips and her fairy fire burned a jealous green as she watched the other pair walk away.

"Next time you can. I'm sure they'll be right back anyways. Then you can watch over her to your little heart's content, okay?" Carey said as she looked the hovering little fairy right in the eyes. "Trust me. Besides, I know Ella. She's super over-protective. She'd never let me go off by myself after what just happened. Plus, the sooner we get the wood we need, the sooner we all get back to camp. Come on."

Mackay huffed and blew a stray curl away from her right eye. She glared at Carey, but no matter how red she turned, her angry looks did not affect Carey. When she decided her temper would not get her what she wanted, she threw up her hands in disgust and decided she had no other choice but to follow. Carey started by picking up fallen branches near the tree line and very soon she had her arms full.

"Mackay, do you think you could scout around for me?" Carey asked.

"Sure," she said, flying ahead. With a flip of an emotional switch, she was pulsing with yellow light. She looked like a flashing beacon each time she found a new stick or branch that was big enough for the fire.

"Fairies must be a lot like toddlers," Carey laughed, mumbling to herself, "they're both easily distracted."

Thirty minutes later the other girls were back, flashlight

leading the way. Lili was swinging her three water bottles and humming to herself, while Ella was managing a fairly large armful of wood she had picked up from along the trail. When they entered the space around the campfire, she dumped her logs and sticks beside the ones Carey had collected, then she dusted off her hands.

"Wow, that's a lot of wood," Ella said, as she admired the large pile the other two had collected in such a short time.

"It's all because of Fairy power!" Mackay boasted, burning bright orange and flexing her tiny muscles, then she added, "Fairies make everything better!"

"Yeah," Ella said with a roll of her eyes before sitting down.

"They also seem a bit full of themselves," Carey remarked to Ella, as she walked up and dumped her last load of wood.

"Whatever. Besides, it's not being proud if it's true," Mackay huffed, poking her nose in the air. She flew over to Lili's shoulder and sat down.

Now that they had collected all the water and firewood they should need for the night, Carey gave everyone a task. "Lili, how about you scrounge around for some snacks? I'm pretty certain I packed some trail mix in my bag somewhere. Just take out whatever looks good. Ella and I'll get the fires going."

Carey grabbed the end of a long stick that was already on

fire and carried it like a torch outside the ring of logs. "Ella, can you grab me a handful of wood, please?"

"Okay, but what are you doing?" Ella asked.

"I'm going to make a few small fires around our camp. The way I figure it, the flames should keep away any unwanted *visitors*," answered Carey. She whispered this just loud enough for Ella to hear her.

"Huh... interesting... where'd you get that idea?" Ella asked, a bit impressed.

"I read about it in a book once. The main characters used fire to keep hungry wolves from attacking them," Carey said, her blue eyes serious. When Ella dropped the load of wood, Carey handed her the torch. The first thing she did was to use a small camp shovel to dig up a circle of grass, then she made a tepee of sticks and small logs. Once all the wood was in place, she took the torch from Ella and placed it right in the middle. With a smile of satisfaction, she said, "That should get it going pretty soon. I'm hoping after we add a few more logs it lasts most of the night."

Carey stood up and scanned the camp's perimeter until she figured out the next spot to put a fire. She wanted to make sure they were in the right places around their camp. "You think you can make a fire like this over on that side?" Carey asked, pointing to where she wanted it. "We'll need at least four fires, one for each opening between the logs."

"Sure thing. I can start the two on that side," Ella said. She stepped over a log and grabbed a large burning branch to start her first fire.

"Thanks," Carey replied.

Soon four new campfires were burning in the four corners of the campsite. They had also built the one in the middle to the size of a bonfire. Its giant flames lit up everything between them and the surrounding trees, but it also made eerie shadows dance on the edge of the darkness.

"Well, at least we have plenty of light! That is, if we don't roast to death!" Lili giggled as she sat down on her sleeping bag. She had just moved it back from the fire, and it was now tucked in tightly besides Ella's. Once she was seated, she set out the things she had found while scrounging. There were Twizzlers, (only half of a bag—she had been sneaking some on the boat when she thought no one was looking), the bag of trail mix Carey had told her about, a container filled with some homemade beef jerky, and Carey's jar of pickles.

"Carey, did you really pack pickles?" Ella laughed, reaching over and grabbing a handful of nuts and dried fruits out of the bag of trail mix.

"Yep, sure did. I never leave home without 'em; that's my camping motto," Carey said as she walked back into the light and sat on the log above her sleeping bag. Ella noticed that she had a few long, straight sticks in her hand. Once she was seated, she pulled her Swiss army knife out of her pocket and began working while the other two snacked. Mackay studied the pickle jar. Without warning, she quickly dipped her tiny finger inside the liquid and then pulled it out and licked it.

Right away Mackay's forehead and face wrinkled in disgust. "Yuck, that tastes horrible! No wonder you people act so funny. How can you eat anything that tastes like that?" Mackay said as she spat and wiped her tongue with her fingers. Her fairy fire began to burn a frustrated purple.

"Oh Mackay, come on, they're not that bad," Carey said, as she whittled her stick. The end was beginning to look quite sharp, a lot like the tip of a spear.

Lili and Ella just laughed at the fairy. Once Ella stopped giggling, she handed Mackay some dried cherries from the trail mix. She figured it might help to cover up the taste of the pickle brine.

"Eat these. They should help," she explained.

"That stuff tastes worse than licking a troll's foot," Mackay complained. Carey raised a questioning brow. "Don't ask. It's a long story," Mackay said. Then she wiped her tongue one last time just for show and started eating the proffered cherries.

When Carey finished her first spear, she rested it against the log she was sitting on and stabbed the tip of her knife blade into the wood. The other girls finished their snacks, and Ella stretched out her arms with clenched fists and released a gigantic yawn.

"Time for bed, everybody. Tomorrow's going to start *really* early," Carey said.

"Okay," Lili yawned. She was too tired to pack up. Her eyes were already blinking and glazed over with sleepiness, so she just slid the bags and jars of food off her sleeping bag. With a yawn, she pulled off her shoes and climbed into her bag. Carey grabbed a few pickles from her jar and a couple strips of beef jerky before she put it all away.

"What about you? Aren't you going to bed?" Lili asked, poking her face back out of her sleeping bag.

"Oh, I'm sure I'll fall asleep sooner or later, but I'm just going to sit up for a while," Carey explained. Ella did not say anything. She preferred to give her older sister a knowing look as she pulled off her shoes and crawled into bed. Carey tried to give her a wink.

"Carey, your eye's twitching again," Ella joked, then added,

"Seriously, wake me up if you need anything, got it?" The stern look on her face and the set of her jaw were clear evidence that she was not playing around.

"Sure thing," Carey said sitting back down, her back propped against the log. "Good night."

"Good night," called out a tiny voice. Carey realized it was Mackay, lying in her nest, her body covered with a large leaf like a blanket and her leg dangling over the side.

"Good night," Lili said weakly from under her covers, and added a late "Mackay" before nodding off to sleep.

Soon everyone else was asleep, but Carey stayed awake. She sat against the log listening to the forest and watching for anything out of the ordinary. She enjoyed the warmth despite the hot night air; it seemed to help. It pushed away the cold she felt inside. She wanted to make sure everyone else was asleep, so she waited until she saw Mackay's fairy fire dim to a faint glow, and then she knew it was safe to let herself cry a good, long, quiet cry. As she did, her shoulders shook, her chest heaved, and her nose ran. As she opened the gates of her heart, all her pent-up pain, confusion, and fear came gushing out, with no stopping at all. Her grief was real and painful, she had only suppressed it in front of her sisters. Afterwards she wiped her nose and dried tired eyes. She was exhausted. All those emotions being released made her feel like a deflated balloon. She wanted to sleep, but she could not let herself. Well, at least not yet. Someone had to watch over them. Someone had to plan. She was determined not to lose anyone else. She could not shake the feeling that if her mother were here, she would be awake and watching over them. *If only she were here...* she started to think. She stopped herself. It took all her will power, but she forced her thoughts away from that dark path. Determined, she picked one of her family's favorite songs and started to hum to herself. Her singing was like defiantly shouting into the darkness when one is afraid to go down in the basement. Maybe you never did that, my reader, but I know I did when I was a kid. As she concentrated on the lyrics and focused her mind, the darkness fell away, and she felt a quiet peace take its place. She wanted to savor it. Now that her mind was clear she was free to plan. *What are we going to do*, she wondered?

After hours of thinking and planning, she was fighting sleep. She fought it as long as she could, but after awhile, it won the war. Little by little her eyes became heavy. They would dip and close ever so slowly as she stared off into the night. Then she would blink her eyes again and again trying to drive the sleep away, but soon enough they would press closed once more. When blinking did not work, she tried rubbing her eyes. When rubbing became useless, she resorted to patting her cheeks. Nothing helped. Her last resort was to splash water in her face, but no matter what she did, the weight of her sleepiness pulled on her. Her mind slowed to a crawl, her head began to nod, and before long, her breathing became calm, slow, and even, and everything felt soft and comfortable. Even the hard log she was leaning against did not help. Without knowing it, she fell asleep, her legs stretched out on her sleeping bag, her spear propped beside her, and the book in her lap. Though her body rested, her mind did not. Her dreams were restless dreams, the kind that come from staying up too late worrying. She relived her plans over and over in those dreams. Each time they tried to rescue her mother, something strange would happen, and her mind would jerk her back to the beginning. There was no real order to it all, but it was a frightening display of failure, and it made her scowl and cringe in her sleep.

CHAPTER 12

Captured

DARKNESS AND CONFUSION SURROUNDED Patty. Her mind was awake, but her body would not move. No matter how hard she tried, she could not open her eyes. Her disembodied thoughts treaded in a deep pool behind her immobile eyelids. The total darkness was disorienting. She longed to break free, to come to the surface of this black pond, but she had no idea how to get there.

As she regained consciousness, she was greeted by pain. Everything ached. Her joints were sore. Cold pain muffled her thoughts. A throbbing stiffness ran up her neck and dug at her shoulders. Her legs were cramped. The cramps took her breath away, so she stopped her futile attempts to move. She just let herself float in the blackness. Lying still seemed to help the pain. Though her eyes remained closed, she could tell that she was lying on her side and pressing down on her wrists. As her body woke up little by little, she was quite aware of her arms. They were stinging with thousands of sharp pin pricks, the type you get after sitting too long when your legs have fallen asleep. The worst part of it was that she could do nothing to relieve her discomfort. For just a moment she felt a strong temptation to go back to sleep. If she was unconscious she would not have to feel so poorly, but she fought this beguiling urge. She knew somehow that she must stay awake. *Where am I?* She was having trouble remembering what had happened. Drugged berries and strong herbs do have a way of doing that to a person.

At this point, all she knew was that she was imprisoned, and until she could open her eyes, even light was denied her. Her only privilege was the sensation of pain. Moments passed in this gloom until she heard something. At least she thought she heard something. It was a low sort of buzzing. Hope made her ears strain to follow it. She fought against the distracting pain, trying to track the source of the noise. It seemed to be her only chance out of this dismal cell. Then the buzzing stopped. *Please, no,* Patty pleaded, *anything is better than this darkness.* But as soon as it stopped, it started again. With each passing note it was more intelligible. It was not buzzing at all, but a kind of humming. It was low, clear, and beautiful. As she listened to each note, she allowed it to pull her closer to the surface, away from the emptiness and towards freedom. It called her to wakefulness like a happy bird calls a person to a sunrise. She thought it sounded like a lullaby or some kind of nursery song. The soft rising and falling of the notes were so comforting and maternal, a strange contrast to her present circumstances. It was like hearing a pallbearer humming a dance tune as he carried a casket in a funeral. The simple tune moved and rolled with a lilt, but she was sure she had never heard it before. Her ears were fully awake now. She could tell that the sound seemed to be closer some moments, and then at others she was certain it was farther away. It was as if the source were moving about.

All at once, a ray of light scattered the darkness. Her eyes fluttered open for the briefest of moments. Her weary mind scrambled for that brightness. It fought to see it again. Hope hung there before her, and she clung to it. This darkness did have an end. The burst of light was followed by a few more flutters of her weak eyelids. At least she knew she could control them. She opened them as wide as she could. The bright light of the morning sun stung her eyes, but for once she did not mind the discomfort. She was not a morning person, but she had never felt so happy to open her eyes and find that the sun was already up. She looked at the immense deep blue sky, the large fluffy white clouds, and reveled in the freedom that they possessed and promised. Maybe after a while she would wish that she had some way to shield her eyes from the rays of the sun, but at that moment she had no desire to do so. Oh, the joy of sunshine after that deep dark pit. My reader, it was like having a loved one switch on a light and hug you after a long bad dream. When she was satisfied, she closed her eyes again. The darkness held no fear for her now that she could open them at will. With her eyes closed, she tried to remember again what had happened to her. As she did, she licked her dry lips, and that was when the humming stopped.

"Well, well. It looks as if mother dearest is finally waking up." The voice that Patty heard was smooth as velvet but laced with sarcasm.

Hearing it, Patty opened her eyes and forced her stiff neck to tilt ever so slightly so she might see who it was. White blonde hairs brushed Patty's cheek, and she saw that a young woman was bending over her. The long strands tickled her nose as the woman moved, but Patty could do nothing about that. Her hands were tied behind her back.

"I hope you slept well," said the full lips with a smile that contained no warmth. The young woman stood and gestured around the camp with her arms stretched out. "Welcome to my new kingdom," she said with a sinister chuckle, "It is not much, but for now, we call it home." Even in Patty's awkward position she was able to look around the camp now that her muscles were working properly.

The camp sat beside a hill with a small cave splitting its side. The hill was half rock and half grass and it wore a crown of wildflowers round its head. The opening in its side was not entirely smooth, but somewhat jagged on one side. It also had a tiny stone outcropping above, like an awning over a door. The lintel was low enough that a tall person would have to stoop before entering. The cave did not look big. It seemed just large enough for a person to lie down in. It would only serve to keep the rain off at best. The floor of the cave was covered with what looked like an old hallway rug, the cheap knock-off kind that pretends to be an expensive Persian. *Aphina definitely has her priorities*, Patty thought. She figured that she must have had some of her minions steal it from one of the empty summer homes that dotted Torch Lake. There were also two sandy brown coyotes near the entrance. They lay there like sentries. One was dozing in the warm sunlight, while its companion on the other side gnawed on a deer bone. The coyotes looked quite content and well fed at the moment.

She was expecting a rebuke, but as she glanced back at Aphina, she noticed a total lack of concern in her eyes. The young woman was quite confident about Patty's current circumstances. She seemed to have nothing to hide. Since Aphina did not care, she let herself look about with open curiosity. As she did, she noticed the camp site was encircled by pine, spruce, and maple trees. In the middle of the camp, not too far from Patty, was a giant fire pit. It was blazing, though it was a hot summer's day. On her left was what looked to be an old fold-up chair. The canvas seat was a little frayed, but it had been set up like a throne, though a shabby one. The copse of trees behind and around it were decorated with two deer skulls and assorted bird feathers. They appeared to have been gathered from the surrounding forest in an attempt to make some type of throne room. Around this throne lay a pack of foxes, their rust-red bodies curled up, with their tails tucked under their heads like pillows. Their black-tipped ears twitched as the flies danced about them. Blinking black lids, like a woman wearing too much eyeliner, drew Patty's attention to the single set of amber eyes that were still open. This one was alert, though it seemed relaxed.

In a corner separated from the pack lay a dog, or maybe it was a wolf. It was a shaggy, matted mess of what must have been at one time a splendid pet. His handsome face was covered with straggly patches of hair, like a prince left to die in a dirty dungeon. His once proud ears were bleeding and nicked, their tips covered with sores made by his swiping claws. Around these, the flies now buzzed and danced incessantly. His high shoulders and thin waist would have been impressive, but the rows of ribs sticking out from his lean body ruined the effect. He sat panting, looking like a strange mix of a faithful house dog and unpredictable wolf. He was half prince and half madman.

Across from the fire pit was an abandoned camp table, the slightly bent aluminum legs holding up a number of glass bottles and an odd assortment of items organized by size and color. *Aphina must have the habit of over packing, like Carey,* thought Patty. In front of the bottles there was a feather pen and a small leather-bound journal with a traveler's inkwell standing open beside it. It looked as if the writer had stopped mid-sentence. In the middle of the table was a small mortar and pestle.

After Patty looked over the table, it seemed as if she had seen all that there was to see, except for the motley flock of birds that sat perched in the tree limbs overhead. That was when she noticed the sleeping badger. He was snoozing near the back table leg. The stripes on his head and the hair of his back were populated more with gray hair than black. Though the creature snored a bit while it slept, Patty was quite sure it still had lots of cranky energy left in its old body.

As Patty finished looking about, the rather tall young woman walked back over to the fire pit. There she stirred the contents of a cooking pot. From the smell that wafted on the breeze, Patty hoped that stuff was not her breakfast. Watching her captor again, she noticed that Aphina was quite slender. Her clothing was not overly worked, but it was cut to accentuate her willowy figure. Her dress was a cobalt blue silk covered with touches of green and gold embroidery. The dress was cut practically, but elegantly. Her slim waist was bound by a leather belt worked with silver studs and intricate scroll work, and on it hung a long serpentine dagger. Aphina's movements were regal, but their precision lent her an air of cool detachment more than of grace and majesty.

"Your wounds are not fatal. You are only scratched and bruised. Consequences of your journey here," Aphina remarked after a time, as she noticed Patty wincing in pain. Her body was fully awake now and there was nothing to mask her discomfort. She could feel every last scrape, cut, and bruise. *Well, you did want to wake up,* Patty thought, reminding herself.

"My stepmother reminded me once that, 'There is no point in crying. It changes nothing,'" Aphina said. Patty noticed that her eye twitched as she quoted those words. "You are safe for now. I have no reason to kill you." She said this as her face returned to a glassy calm. After a short pause she added, "Not yet, anyway."

As Patty tried to sit up (which is very hard to do with one's arms tied behind one's back), she spooked an overly curious squirrel that was sniffing her shoes. She could not stifle her groans as she pushed herself upright. Picking up a silver flask from the camp table, Aphina walked over. She unscrewed the cap and pressed it to her lips. "Drink. We must keep up our strength, mustn't we?"

Patty refused it at first. She fought the urge to gulp it down. Her throat was parched, but with determined blue eyes, she stared at her captor. She was trying to discern this young woman's intentions.

"Well, we are a spirited one. Not very trusting, are we? I like that. Don't worry. It's not poisoned or drugged. See?" Aphina tasted some of the water and then offered it to Patty again. This time Patty drank it. She tried not to appear greedy, but the cool water was tempting. After a dozen or so deep swallows, she managed to empty the whole flask. When she was done, Aphina pulled it back and capped it again.

Right then, her crow flew over and perched on Aphina's shoulder. He cawed as she turned away. "No, Byrne, my pet," Aphina said, scratching under the bird's beak with a manicured nail, "I think there is no need to muzzle this one. Who is she going to call?"

The crow's beady black eyes searched the surrounding forest. His head pivoted back and forth, then he flapped his wings once and cawed as if speaking to his mistress.

"The children are of no consequence. Soon enough I will discover how to use my powers to their full extent in this strange land, and *then* no one will be able to stop me." She said this as she picked up her feather pen and jotted down an idea. As for her crow, he flew to a sagging branch just above the table. When she had finished writing, Aphina turned and looked at Patty. Her words were laced with disdain and her eyes were filled with what almost looked like pity. For all her royal ways, she looked like a haughty nursemaid explaining the ways of the world to a spoiled, naïve little child. "See, mother dearest, your children are weak. They have been made soft with kindness and love. They have been pampered with years of affection, like I once was," Aphina said, then paused as she laid her index finger across her mouth. Tapping her lips, she inspected Patty. After the briefest inspection of her prey, she removed her finger and spoke again. "Right about now they are awakening to the shocking realities of life. *'Mommy is gone. What will we do?'*" She spoke in mocking tones, mimicking a child's frightened voice, then with utter confidence she added, "No, they are no threat. They are weak! Love does not build; it binds! It ensnares the soul with impossible dreams and fairy stories," she spat out these last words as she clenched her open hand into a fist. "They have no idea how to harness the cold harsh pain that they will need to overcome me. Their fears will come stalking them! They will keep them at bay," Aphina said with mocking tones. With each passing word she had taken a menacing step closer to Patty. Her face was a cold mask of confidence, though as she drew closer and bent to stare into her eyes, Patty thought she saw pain hidden behind all that steely resolve.

After that speech Patty decided it would be unwise to speak, but that did not mean she was going to consider Aphina's lies.

Her blue eyes blazed in defiance. The arrogance and conceit of this woman had riled Patty's stubborn streak. As her anger boiled just below the surface she thought, *Your world may be dark, but hope still lives here.* Grinding her teeth, Patty forced herself to smile. She would not let this young woman see her fear. She would not let these doubts creep into her mind, to lodge in her heart, so that they might chip away at her resolve and courage. As she refused to cower before this darkness, a glimmer of hope rose in her heart. It came as she remembered again the very words she had said to her daughter the day before: "When you are afraid, think truth, for truth has nothing to be afraid of."

As Aphina watched for the natural fear and hopelessness her words should produce, her confidence was checked for an instant. *I am right; my reasoning faultless,* she thought, *so why is this helpless woman smiling?* With that question came a sliver of doubt. *What unknown hope could she be clinging to? What secret does she hold that helps her stand against my wisdom? She has no power, no army, and no might. So, what is it?* she wondered. Then a thought came to her that she had not considered before. *The book, yes... the book, that must be it. Those contemptible weak children still have that cursed book. It must contain strong magic if it can bind a sorceress like me,* Aphina thought, her eye twitching again. *Well, that little problem should be easy enough to remedy, shouldn't it?* she thought. A confident smile returned to Aphina's face as she turned away from her prisoner.

Patty at last let out the breath she had been holding, that is, once she was certain Aphina's back was turned. It had taken everything, all her strength to hold that smile in the face of this woman and the darkness she exuded, but it had worked. Somehow her defiance had shaken something. It might not have been much, but something had shifted. She had seen its impact just for a second in Aphina's eyes, but she had no idea the extent of that hidden wound. She did not know that she had found the chink in Aphina's pretentious armor of indifference. Hope, after all, my reader, is the greatest enemy of bitterness. But what she did know was that she had to keep on fighting. Sooner or later she might find a way out.

"Byrne," Aphina cried to her crow. As she bellowed, he perked up and stood at attention. "Gather your followers. Take all the birds and visit our little friends. Get that book and bring it here," she commanded. "And do not fail me, Byrne." These last words were whispered, but they were filled with a menace more effective than any shouting.

With raucous cawing, the crow called his underlings. Patty

watched as the surrounding tree branches swayed with the beating of a multitude of wings. A murder of crows, a congress of sleepy owls, and the castoffs of the hawks rose from their seats. They would obey the demands of their new master at any cost, Patty was quite certain.

CHAPTER 13

The Best Laid Plans...

BACON FRYING. THAT WAS WHAT WOKE Carey. She heard it sizzling. She smelled its salty greasy goodness before she opened her eyes. For a few seconds, she lay on her sleeping bag savoring the scent and relishing the thought of it before her dream faded away. It had all been so real. The best dreams are like that, my reader. Just moments before, she had been in the kitchen with her mother and father. They had been enjoying a normal pleasant morning. Besides the sights and sounds of home dancing in a blur before her eyes, her active imagination had been more than happy to intermingle the surrounding smells into her dreams. It was disappearing now, but her tongue was still watering. She could almost swear that she could smell the scents of maple syrup and melted butter lingering in the air. Maybe, just maybe, if she squeezed her eyes tight enough, she might find a way back into that wonderful dream. She could go back to that world where her whole family had been cooking her favorite breakfast. She could find the way back down the tunnel that led to the place where her life was simple again, where everything was perfect, where her morning started with a plate of pancakes and bacon.

She stretched and yawned. She blinked. Then she saw Ella sitting over the small cast iron skillet. Her sister was the one doing the cooking. All her fancies dissolved like the night sky does before the warm light of the rising sun. Disappointed, she realized her mom and dad were not laughing and flirting while they made pancakes in the kitchen.

"Oh, it's you," Carey said in a voice that made her sound like a grumpy toad, glaring from the underside of a lily pad. She scrunched her eyes shut once again, but sleep would not return. There was nothing else to do but sit up.

"Thanks. Good morning to you, too!" Ella said, flipping the bacon.

In a moment or two, the fog in her muddled brain was gone. The memories of the day before came crashing back into Carey's mind. *I can't believe you fell asleep,* she scolded herself. She jumped up, and grabbed the things she had been working on the night before. "Where's Lili?" Carey demanded, worry filling her as she looked around.

"Calm down, Carey. She's right over there," Ella said, pointing with the fork she was using. Carey turned to see their sister. She was playing among the trees that lined the path to the meadow. "I told her she couldn't go too far," Ella explained as she pulled the last pieces of bacon out of the pan and took the pan off the fire. She called out, "Breakfast is ready!"

Carey let out a frustrated sigh.

"Carey, stop beating yourself up. You know nobody in our family ever gets up before Lili, not even dad. She was up chirping like a bird at the crack of dawn. She woke me up while she was getting out of bed, so we decided to get a few things packed and ready. It's really no biggy. You know she's never satisfied until she can get some food in her belly."

"Yeah, but I'm the oldest," Carey protested.

"Look, Carey," Ella said, "It's okay. You're doing great." Almost an entire minute elapsed until Ella's next words broke the uncomfortable silence. "I know you stayed up *really* late last night planning and watching over us. So, I figured a few minutes of extra sleep were the least you deserved." As she spoke, she placed the food on the metal dishes. Each plate held pieces of bacon, a boiled egg, and a banana. "Sorry about breakfast; it's all I could find. Those dumb animals must have eaten every last thing they could smell."

Carey finally swallowed her pride. It was bitter as it went down, but there was nothing else to do but to accept the fact that she had slept in. With effort, she let it go, then she smiled at her sister. "The breakfast looks fine. At least we still have the eggs. The three of 'em together sound a whole lot better than just bacon and bananas," She said with a slight chuckle.

"By the way...thanks. You know, for trying to take care of us," Ella said as she handed Carey her plate. "You're a good big sister," she added. She had a way of breaking her sentences into little pieces when she was trying to express her deepest feelings. It was not that Ella did not try to communicate her feelings, it was just that sometimes everything seemed to get all tangled up when she tried to let it all out.

Carey smiled and nodded. Taking her plate, she called for her sister again. "Lili, breakfast's ready!"

Lili heard them the second time and came running. Mackay delayed for a moment, then she came zipping up behind her. Carey noticed that Lili had a serious case of bed head, and Mackay's fairy fire flickered dimly. Carey figured that meant she was only half-awake. Though they were both a crumpled mess, they looked quite ready for breakfast.

"I'm starving," Lili said, grabbing her plate.

"You're always hungry," Ella retorted.

"Yeah, but today, I'm *really* hungry," Lili explained.

Ella handed Mackay her small plate, but the fairy looked at it with skeptical eyes. "It's bacon. You know, pig meat that's smoked? Then there's an egg. You've got to know what boiled eggs are, and the yellow thing is a banana."

"Banana? What's that?" Mackay asked as she sat down next to Lili. Her fairy fire snapped and crackled, matching the pop of her sarcasm. "You people are so strange. Who eats foods named ba-na-na?" Mackay said with a laugh, stressing all the syllables of the last word.

"Just eat," Ella said.

Everyone enjoyed the distraction that eating provided. Soon enough it was over, and Lili was collecting the plates while Carey and Ella decided what needed to be done next.

"I made two more spears this morning and packed our bags before I started breakfast. I figured that much out. But I didn't have a clue about how we're going to find mom. We don't know a thing about following trails or tracking stuff," Ella said.

"I think I have that part figured out. I spent a lot of time thinking last night," Carey said. "Here, look at this," she added, opening the book where she had left her bookmark. Pointing at the illustration, she said, "I think she can help us."

Her finger was resting on a picture of a Native American girl riding on the back of a white buffalo. The night sky above them was filled with shimmering stars and the subtle bands of the Milky Way. The buffalo was thundering across the foreground as the wind whipped the girl's raven black braids behind her. In their wake, the Northern Lights rippled and formed the pictures of different animals.

"You sure she'll help?" Ella asked.

"Well, I figure she's our best bet right now. I skimmed through most of the stories last night before I fell asleep. I even made a list of creatures that might help us once we find Aphina's camp. We might even read out a few dragons to light things up," Carey said, smiling as she imagined them swooping in and saving the day. "But we have to find the camp first, and I think this girl is the only one that can help us do that."

"Who is she?" asked Lili as she walked over after finishing her job. She was supposed to wash dishes this morning, but boiled eggs, bananas, and bacon are not that hard to clean up.

"Her name's Alsoomse. The story says she's a Piegan Blackfoot. Her mother died before she was four years old, and her father refused to remarry. The legend said that his wife was more beautiful than the setting sun. He lived in her teepee and raised their daughter alone," Carey explained, punctuating it all with a school-girl sigh. "When old enough, she chose to learn the work of a warrior. Some of the men scorned her father, but he didn't care. She learned hunting, trapping, and tracking, but in time the elders also advised him to let the women in the village teach her 'women's work.' If he did not, they feared no man would be willing to marry her."

"But why would she help us?" Ella asked.

"Just let me finish the story, Ella. Not long after the elders met with her father, the village moved to Marias River. The first winter many of her people got sick and died. One day while the men were out hunting, government soldiers came and attacked the village. Alsoomse was fetching water when the attack began. The book said she was wounded by a bullet, but she tried to sneak around the camp to get her weapons anyways. The pain was so great it caused her to pass out and she fell into an old buffalo wallow. Nahtoosi, that's their Creator God, was said to have sent a pure white female bison to her to keep her warm as she lay there unconscious. After a while she woke up again and saw smoke coming from the village. When she tried to get up, she passed out again because she had lost so much blood. The legend said that the buffalo changed its form and became a kind old woman who made a shelter out of buffalo hides and took care of Alsoomse by bandaging her wounds. When she woke, her wound was healed and only a scar remained. Before her eyes the old woman turned into the white buffalo. When she finally returned to the village, everyone was gone, even her father. Everyone had either been taken away or killed. The grief was overwhelming. For a long time Alsoomse couldn't understand why Nahtoosi had spared her. But what she did know was that from that day forward the white buffalo refused to leave her. It was like some kind of guardian or protector, or something. With the buffalo's help, she ran off to join the Northern Blackfoot Tribes in Canada. She wanted them to be her new people. When she arrived, the people marveled at her story. They had never seen a young woman who could use the bow and spear as she could, let alone a woman who was followed around by a sacred white buffalo. Some in the tribe were afraid of her. They even asked her to be sent away, but the presence of the guardian influenced the chief and council. In the end, she was allowed to stay. When she reached the age that she would be allowed to marry, she was said to have been visited in a dream. Nahtoosi came to her and told her she had been saved to help others. That is when she decided to leave the village and become a wanderer. The tribes only saw her from time to time, going and coming. They believed she traveled through the forests and prairies in search of lost people and helpless children. She was trying to fulfill the wish of the Creator by helping them."

"Wow, kinda weird....but if she can help us, that's great." Ella said.

"I think the Blackfoot girl's a great idea, but I got a question," said Lili, "Are her feet really black?"

"No goof-ball, that's just a tribal name that the settlers gave them," Carey answered, rolling her eyes. "Well, if all the votes are in?" Everyone nodded in agreement and Carey added, "I'll read."

Carey sat down next to the two small backpacks that Ella had prepared earlier that morning. Each girl laid her spear on the log next to her. Even Mackay stopped flying about and sat on Lili's shoulder. She looked dressed and ready for adventure. During the girls' conversation, she had flown to her nest and replaced her rumpled clothes with new ones. They were made of fresh green leaves and bound together with grass stems and tiny vines. As Ella looked her over, she figured the clothes would not do her much good as camouflage. The very first time Mackay felt happy—or felt anything for that matter—she would light up like a neon signboard. Her fairy fire would shout to anybody looking, "Hey you! I'm over here, look at me!" But Ella decided to keep her comments to herself. After all, Mackay's little face was beaming with an excited grin, and her fairy fire was burning with an eager white flame. *Why spoil the moment?* With one final look at Lili and Ella, Carey placed the open book in her lap. Ella crossed her fingers, and Lili scooched a little closer to her sister. Taking a deep breath, Carey began to read...

"The earth shook with the thunder of hooves. At the front of the herd was Alsoomse, the helper of the lost, sitting on the broad shoulders of her white buffalo. She looked like a carving on the prow of a ship, her straight form jetting out from the crest of the stampeding wave. The rolling swell about her was made of hundreds of buffalo surging over the open plain. She felt the power of the buffalo below her, she felt the wind as it clutched at her. It sent her long ebony braids over her shoulders to snap in the air behind her. From deep within, her emotions rose. They would not be suppressed. She laughed, but the peals of joy were swallowed up by the rumbling of the hooves. Overwhelmed, she screamed into the wind, her cries thrown into the clear blue sky above. Breathing deeply, she inhaled the fresh air of freedom after a long

confining winter. The midday sun kissed her skin. There was no need for her warm beaded coat this fine spring day, so she was clad in her lighter buckskin dress and lowcut black moccasins. Triumphantly, she raised her bare arms to the wind. She felt like a bird about to take flight. She was alive; she was free. She knew this was the life for her. The thoughts then came sweeping into her mind: wide open plains, the last of the buffalo herds, freedom to follow the will of Nahtoosi..."

Carey stopped reading as a cool breeze caressed her cheek. Then the silence was filled with the rumble of buffalo hooves. It rolled into the clearing like the sounds of distant thunder. Puffs of dust ascended from the edges of the page. The air around them filled with the fine brown particles, and they coughed as it filled their noses and mouths. It was like standing beside a dirt road as a speeding truck flies by. There was clear fresh air, then the next moment, everything was a cloud of dust. As Lili scrunched her eyes closed and Ella held her nose, the dust settled. Shimmers of light like the Aurora Borealis rose from the open page. They were a kaleidoscope of colors, shining like a thousand rainbow hues on the surface of a soap bubble. As it rose, one part, a blue glistening light, floated away from the rest. As it undulated and pulsed, it formed the shape of a flying hawk. Its wings spread and it soared over their heads. Without warning, its shrill cry pierced the sky. Another, shimmering green and yellow, broke away and the form of an elk emerged in its light. Its great antlered head reared back, and it bugled its long wailing call. The last and largest wave of light grew, rippling into strands of red, yellow, and orange. As it shook, it formed one mighty buffalo. The girls watched in awe as its massive head and shoulders rose with a grunt and then lowered as it pawed the ground. Its nostrils flared wide, and it exhaled a blast of hot steamy breath into their faces. As they blinked, Alsoomse appeared. She simply stepped through the swirling patterns of mist and lights. Before them she stood, firm and tall, and looked at them with dark, staring eyes.

CHAPTER 14

Going Hunting

VERYONE SAT WAITING, AND THEN ELLA worked up her courage. Standing, she raised her hand into the air as if she were asking a question in class, then with great ceremony she exclaimed, "*How!*"

Alsoomse looked puzzled. Then she rolled her eyes at the girl standing before her.

Carey shoved her sister aside, and said with a scowl, "Really?"

"Maybe she only speaks Blackfoot-ese," Lili offered innocently from her seat on the log.

"Yes, I am Blackfoot, but we call ourselves the Nizitapi," said Alsoomse. "But I speak the English, though your words are different from those of the traders and missionaries I have met. My people call me Alsoomse."

"Our people call us Carey, Ella, and Lili," Carey said, pointing to each girl. "We are sisters. We are from the place called Michigan."

Carey was quite happy Mackay had chosen this moment to feel shy. All the dust and lights must have frightened her, because she was more than content to hide behind Lili's shoulder. Carey was not sure how she was going to explain the fairy to Alsoomse.

As the girls inspected Alsoomse, she inspected the camp. Carey thought she looked a bit older than herself. Her face was very pretty, though her arms had bigger muscles than any boys Carey knew. Her movements were graceful and smooth, like an elegant dancer. As Carey watched her, she noticed the way Alsoomse stood balanced on her toes, how she always kept the girls in the corner of her vision no matter where she looked. She appeared 'ready'—at least that was the word Carey could think of to describe it. It reminded her of their cat back home. Whenever Butter was about to pounce on something, his body would become all fluid movements. He would hunker down, his eyes would become intent and focused, and his tail would begin to swish back and forth. Sometimes he would decide to attack and sometimes he would go back to licking his paws, but one knew by watching him that he was ready. Carey was certain that this young lady was always ready for a fight. Ella, on the other hand, felt that Alsoomse reminded her of one of the mama swans at the city park. They were beautiful and majestic, but it was going to be a bad day for anyone that got too close to their baby cygnets. If the mother felt threatened, she would use her powerful wings and practically knock the head off of anyone close by. Both sisters felt weak and clumsy compared to this girl. The one comfort though was that her serious face held very kind eyes.

"Please, will you sit with us?" Carey asked, as she sat down and motioned for her sisters to do the same.

Alsoomse sat easily; it was obvious she was used to strange situations.

"We called you here to help us," Ella interjected. She was uncomfortable waiting on Carey to find her words.

"You 'called' me *here*?" Alsoomse asked with a confused expression. She looked around again as if to discover what the girl meant by the word 'here.'

"Ella!" Carey said quietly but firmly, placing her hand on her sister's knee. Then she took the lead. "Yes, we need help. See, our father is on a journey for a time, he has gone away…"

Carey hesitated, but she could not see any normal way to explain it, so she finally jumped right in, "and a witch, I think you use the term medicine woman, or shaman, has stolen our mother from us. We don't know how to find her."

"So you have brought me 'here,' beyond the great waters to Michigan, so I can help you find your lost mother?" Alsoomse asked.

"Yes," Ella said interrupting again in her eagerness.

"I see," said Alsoomse, "I would ask one question."

"Okay, shoot," Carey replied without thinking.

Alsoomse looked confused, then looked into the woods for any threat she might have overlooked.

"Sorry," Carey explained, feeling slightly embarrassed. "It's just an expression here, it means, go ahead and ask your question. There isn't anything to shoot at or anything trying to shoot at us."

"Yes, I understand now," Alsoomse said, pausing to think over her question, "If you have the power to bring me here, why do you need my help to find this medicine woman?"

"Well, that's a good question," Carey said linking her fingers together, and twiddling her thumbs self-consciously. Then she said, "Alsoomse, we're not really sure how you got here. It's a bit hard to explain."

"Yeah, it's complicated," Ella added.

"It's kind of like a miracle," Lili explained.

"A miracle," Alsoomse said, testing the word. "I have heard a missionary use this word many years ago in my village. He said it is a thing of the Creator God."

"Well, how you got here was definitely creative," Ella said tentatively, before Carey elbowed her and she stopped talking.

"If it is the will of Nahtoosi, then he asks me to obey without question. I was spared to serve the helpless, so I will help you."

"Great," they all said at once, even Mackay, who decided right at that moment to come out of hiding. Once she did, she sprang from behind Lili like a Jack coming out of his box. Then she fluttered above Lili's head, shining with bright yellow fairy fire.

"Tsá?" Alsoomse exclaimed in Blackfoot. She was clearly not used to being surprised.

"This is Mackay," Lili offered by way of explanation. "She's a fairy."

Alsoomse seemed to be clutching at something hanging about her neck under her buffalo skin shirt. She loosened her grip when she noticed that the little creature was content to smile at her and hover harmlessly by the girls.

Then, without any warning, Mackay flew straight at the

young woman's face. Stopping in mid-air a few inches away from her nose, Mackay stood staring. The girls were shocked that Alsoome was so composed and had not swatted at her like a giant buzzing mosquito.

"I've never seen anyone like you before," Mackay said openly, inspecting Alsoomse's beautiful copper skin and deep walnut brown eyes.

"I have never seen a *fairee*," Alsoomse said, struggling with the new word. Carey noticed that for the first time she had a girlish sort of wonderment in her eyes. She was awed as she inspected the fairy, who spun about slowly with grand motions, making faces like a pampered princess. Each little circle was made so that Alsoomse could admire Mackay's wings and clothing to their fullest extent. "Your fairee has beautiful wings like a butterfly," commented Alsoomse at last, "I, of all people, should know that Nahtoosi's helpers come in many forms."

Mackay's fairy fire leaped from her in hundreds of tiny crackling orange lines, the compliment making her ignite like a sparkler. She looked for all the world like a burning little sun trying to blind their eyes with her intensely blazing pride.

When Mackay's light dimmed, Alsoomse added, "I greet you, butterfly child, helper of Nahtoosi." She said this with respect and a bow of her head.

"I greet you, Alsoomse," said Mackay with a grave bow, then, in a total change of character Mackay began to stomp and growl in mid-air doing some kind of fairy warrior dance around Alsoomse's head.

While Alsoomse laughed at Mackay's childishness, Carey and Ella got their backpacks on and picked up their spears. They were more than ready to get started.

"Now that everyone knows each other, let's get going," Carey suggested, pointing over to the tracks left by the animals the day before, "the trail starts there."

Alsoomse walked over to inspect the ground. She spent time looking at each print and placing her fingers into many of them. The girls stood watching her with interest. They tried to give her room to think without any distractions. Lili thought that the time was right, so she grabbed Carey's hand and pulled it twice.

"Carey, may I carry the book, please?"

"You really want to?" Carey asked.

"Yes! Alsoomse can have my spear. I promise I'll be *really* careful," Lili pleaded. Her sister knew she really wanted to help.

"Okay, but don't get it wet or dirty. Got it?"

"I promise. Cross my heart and hope to die... I won't get it wet or dirty," Lili said as she crossed her chest with her index finger.

When Carey got the book out of the bag and handed it to Lili, she clutched it. She held it like an ancient relic, gripping it firmly in both hands. They turned their attention to Alsoomse, who had finished inspecting the prints.

"The trail is a day old, but it will not be hard to follow. The animals are in a mixed pack: coyotes, foxes, and maybe a dog or wolf. It is strange that they run together," Alsoomse paused, looking slightly puzzled. "They dragged your mother off on some kind of blanket, but there is no blood. Let us go. I hope she is not far," Alsoomse said, finishing her thought. Without hesitation or another word, she grabbed the spear offered to her by Carey and walked off into the woods. It appeared that she expected the girls to follow her.

Thirty minutes later the group was tromping along in a straggling line down one of the old camping trails. Alsoomse turned every few minutes and placed her fingertip over her closed mouth and raised her eyebrows. She wanted them to be quieter, though they were trying to be as quiet as they knew how. Carey had even heard Alsoomse mumble to herself that they sounded like a herd of buffalo walking by.

At first the path they followed had been a narrow game trail, but the tracks had abruptly turned left when they had crossed a larger hiking path. The path was spacious, but overgrown.

The grass was longer than it should have been and dotted with wildflowers. There were no more rangers to keep the trail mowed, but the overhanging trees blocked most of the sunlight so the grass was more of a shaggy carpet with a few wild patches of overgrowth. The most encouraging part of their trip thus far was the fact that even though the animals had dragged their mother the entire way, Alsoomse saw no sign of a blood trail. She had assured them that they were taking their mother some place, but it did not appear that they intended to hurt her, at least for the moment. The girls were rejoicing over this bit of good news and chewing on its implications when Alsoomse abruptly stopped.

"The animals stopped here for a rest. They must have been very tired. This *Skin-walker* must have strong medicine. I have never seen a pack drag something this far without killing and eating it."

Ella tried to see what Alsoomse was talking about on the ground, but except for an occasional paw print, she could not see anything different about this spot compared to the tracks they had followed the last thirty minutes.

"What makes you so sure?" she asked.

"Look here," Alsoomse pointed, "see how the grass is pressed flat? It is not just bent; it has been laid on by something for some time. See the two straight lines leading to it?" Ella looked at the marks on the ground with interest. Alsoomse helped her by tracing two long lines of leaves and twigs that formed wakes in the grass caused by the animals dragging her mother's sleeping body. "Your mother's body was pulled until here. All the animal tracks are pulling, see? The print here is deep," she said as she pointed back up the trail, but then walked over to the impressions in the dirt nearest to them and said, "but here they stopped to rest. They are very tired." Watching Alsoomse, Ella could see a little bit of what she meant. "After rest, they began to move about and to walk in circles and the tracks are... thin," Alsoomse said, looking for the right word.

"I guess I see, but you still don't see any blood, right?" Ella asked, concerned.

"No, she is not wounded, but I think she will be..." she paused to consider the words, "will be *unhappy* when she wakes," she explained, making a sign with her hands. It and the expression on her face let the girls know what she meant. Their mother would be very sore when she woke up. "I do not think it should be too far now. Come and we go. The forest seems too quiet now; I do not like it."

Alsoomse picked up her spear again and started down the trail as Carey and Lili closed their water bottles. With the pace Alsoomse set, the girls took every opportunity they could to take a sip from their canteens. Suddenly, from above the canopy came a chorus of strange sounds, and all eyes peered up through the receding tree line above the path. Bursting through the opening like an exploding firecracker came a flock of hawks, owls, and crows. They opened their beaks in a cacophony of hoots, screeches, and caws, a confused chorus of cries. The girls stood wide-eyed as the birds drew in their wings and dove.

"Run!" Carey screamed. "Get under the trees," she cried, almost dropping her spear. Ella hesitated, but Lili quickly ran after her older sister. Mackay fought all her fairy instincts that were demanding that she abandon Lili, and somehow she managed to stay right above her shoulder.

"Stop running and fight them," Alsoomse cried as she dodged a crow and sprinted across the path, landing a blow on a hawk that was approaching Ella. The spear shaft caught the animal near its head with a thwack.

"What are we supposed to do?" Ella pleaded, trying to get as close as she could to Alsoomse, who was swinging her spear in every direction. Her fighting was calm, smooth, and deadly. Two birds already lay wounded on the path. Ella, on the other hand was swinging wildly at the swooping attackers with one hand, while attempting to cover her face and eyes with the other.

"Watch and move fast," Alsoomse commanded, knocking a hawk out of the air with a crushing blow.

Carey was farthest into the trees and swinging her spear like a crazed baseball player with a bat. Most of the crows were attacking her, but at least she was keeping them at bay. Somehow, she had even managed to wound one large gray owl. It had retreated to a nearby tree branch so that it might watch the show. As it rested its wounded wing, it hooted encouragement to its companions from time to time.

Lili was caught in the middle, absolutely helpless without her spear, screaming. Her high-pitched shriek echoed in the surrounding trees. The first owl that swooped by her startled her so much that she stopped screaming and started crying. To give her credit, my reader, Lili had more pluck than she knew, and very soon her cries of fear were mixed with tears of anger. She was all alone and blocked on either side by both owls and crows. She did not know whether to use the book as a shield or a weapon. She already had a few scrapes and cuts on her arms from owl claws that burned hotly and were starting to bleed, but she was trying her best not to lose her wits. Mackay's fairy fire burned a deep blue as she hid behind Lili's shoulders, below her bobbing ponytail. When Carey saw her sister's predicament, she tried to press forward to reach her. Then she saw her younger sister bend over to grab a stick from off the ground.

"Go away, you nasty birds!" Lili screamed as she stood. She tried to club a crow with her newly acquired weapon, but a great horned owl swooped low and rammed into her. It was like being hit by a dodge ball when not expecting it. The force knocked her to the ground. Lili fell with a hard thud, the book slipped from her fingers, and it went tumbling end over end to rest a few feet away. The wind had been knocked out of her, and she was gasping for breath in the dirt. Her chest filled with painful spasms. Pulling herself up with one hand, she clutched at her chest with the other, until she finally felt air begin to fill her lungs again. Furiously she blinked the tears from her eyes. The pain seemed to make her angry and sad all at the same time. As she inspected herself, she discovered that she had scrapes on her hands from the rough stones on the path. Once she saw them, they stung, adding to her overall discomfort.

Rage seized Carey as she broke through the circling crows and felled two birds. They were killed by a crushing blow before they even touched the ground. Running up, she swung her spear in a blind fury and landed a home run swing on the great horned owl that had hopped over to snap at her sister's back. The owl's body bent with a crunch, absorbing the blow, and sailed through the air crashing into a nearby tree. Lili scrambled to her feet with help from Carey. There they stood, back to back, swinging their sticks at the remaining birds. The birds were circling them like hungry sharks around a stranded lifeboat. All this time Mackay was tucked between their shoulder blades. From time to time she would pop out, shake her fist at their attackers and call down fairy curses on their feathery heads. Her body blazed with a light as red as a fire engine.

Alsoomse and Ella had killed all the hawks but were still fighting with a flock of crows when Ella looked over at Carey and cried, "Carey, the book!"

Carey looked to Lili's empty hands, and then searched frantically around. "Where's the book?" she shouted.

"I don't know... I dropped it when I fell," Lili yelled while swinging wildly at a swooping bird.

A second too late Carey realized the reason Ella had yelled. Aphina's big black crow and two large owls were standing over the book trying to get hold of the leather straps that bound it together. The crow was in front, as if he was telling them what to do. The two owls were near the top and bottom. Each owl sunk its talons beneath the taut straps and braced themselves to haul the book away. All this time they were cawing and hooting back and forth as if talking. After a long caw from the crow that almost seemed like a command to pull, the owls flapped their large wings with all their effort.

"No!" Carey cried as she ran for the book, but at that moment an owl sensed her distraction. Taking its chances, it struck at her, cutting a gash in her outstretched hand. The book was lost from her sight in the confusion of flapping wings and searing pain. Carey jerked back her wounded hand just as Lili smacked the gloating bird with her stick.

Within a few moments Alsoomse had at last killed the attackers that remained on her side. In fact, she had pierced the final two crows at the exact same time. They collided, trying to evade an erratic swing of Ella's spear. Their mistake was their misfortune.

Now that the path between the two parties was clear, Alsoomse and Ella ran over to Carey and Lili. Many of the birds that had attacked them littered the ground, though there were a few very persistent crows that would not give up the fight. They continued their sweeping attacks with raucous cries. They acted like ugly bullies who chuckled as they kicked the kid that was down, though in true bully fashion they went running when help was on its way. With angry squawks of protest the birds flew off. The droning of their 'caaww, caaww, caaww,' echoed in the canopy above. With the departure of these final foes, the spears and sticks were at last lowered and everyone stood panting. As the spinning feathers settled and the burning of their wounds decreased, the girls realized the book had been taken. Their loss was profound. The book was gone, and they did not know what to do. It had been their hope. They had built all their plans upon it.

"No one looks to be dying. The wounds are small," Alsoomse said.

"Yeah," said Carey, clutching her bleeding arm, "but they got the book."

"Lili, what happened?" shouted Ella in an explosion of anger. "How'd you lose the book?" The look in her eyes as she glared at her little sister was a whirlwind of fear and frustration.

Lili's shoulders stooped, her eyes welled up with tears, and her lip quivered, "I'm sorry, I—I didn't mean to drop it," Lili explained. She stumbled over her words. "When that bird hit me, it, it just flew out of my hands."

"Great job! Now what are we gonna do?" Ella shouted, her face red and her voice harsh.

Lili turned away from her sisters and hurled her stick into the woods, then she bolted like a frightened deer. She just wanted to find a tree big enough to cry behind. Mackay frowned angrily at Ella. Her fairy fire blazed like a red-hot ember as she flew off after Lili.

"Ella, come on, how about you calm down a little! You're acting like she handed the book to the crows on purpose. Besides, I didn't see you coming to save the day," Carey rebuked her annoyed sister.

Carey could tell by the teardrops creeping into the corners of Ella's eyes that her words were caused more by fear than by true anger. Ella never was very good with surprises. For a moment Ella stood there on the brink of tears. Her chest was heaving. Then she raised her arms in the air and swung them about like an angry basketball coach ranting at his losing team. "Carey, that book was our only hope! Now what are we going to do?! How do we get Mom back, huh?" Ella shouted. After she had vented all her emotions, Ella let her hands fall with a thump against her legs.

"I think I will go and scout ahead. After, I will return," Alsoomse said quietly. She cast a sympathetic look at the girls, and then turned and trotted up the path.

"Look, Ella," Carey said as she grabbed her sister's shoulders and made her look her in the eyes. Carey knew her sister well enough not to be shaken by her temper. "Mom *is* in danger, but we are *not* helpless. She's counting on us, and I am *not* going to stand around and watch us fight with each other. That's just what Aphina wants. We have to stick together," she said, trying to kindle some inspiration in her sister. "As for our plan, we'll figure something out. Mom told me back at Eastport that our duty was to follow the truths we already know."

After a moment or two of silence, Ella breathed out a long, frustrated sigh. "Fine, but what do we do now?" Ella asked, looking up at her sister. It appeared that her emotions were at least simmering instead of boiling over.

"Well, for starters, how about you go over and apologize to our little sister for biting her head off. It really wasn't her fault. You know it was a mistake," Carey suggested as she pointed towards Lili. They both looked to where Lili sat with her knees pulled up, her back against a tree. Her head was down and tucked behind her folded arms. Mackay's somber green fairy fire burned like a mournful halo around Lili's head from where the fairy sat on her opposite shoulder.

Ella bit her lip as she walked over to where her sister was hiding. She sat down on the damp mossy ground next to Lili and touched her knee. Lili pulled back from her touch and scooched a few inches away. Frowning, she turned her shoulder and glowered at the twig she was holding. Silent tears were running down her cheeks. As the seconds ticked by and Ella thought over her words, she watched as Lili snapped off tiny pieces from the twig she held in her hands.

"I'm sorry, Lili," confessed Ella at last. While she spoke, she tried to shoo Mackay away. The fairy had her little face scrunched into a scowl, and she glared at Ella. It seemed as if her whole face burned with a bright red flame. "Please go away? I'll deal with this," Ella mouthed at Mackay. After patting Lili's head and giving Ella a curt huff, Mackay finally flew away.

Ella placed her hand on Lili's knee once again, then bent close to her sister's ear and whispered softly, "I know it wasn't your fault..."

"You said it was," Lili cut in angrily.

"I'm sorry. I was angry. Losing the book was just an accident," Ella said. Each sentence was followed by a brief pause as Ella felt for her words. "It could've happened to anyone. Lili, please forgive me."

Lili wiped her nose on her arm, but she did not answer. She was thinking.

"Truth is, I only got angry because I'm scared," Ella admitted. "I want to get Mom back and get this whole thing over with."

Without warning, Lili reached over and grabbed her sister's arm in a tight squeeze. Ella squeezed her back. After a few moments, Lili mumbled to her older sister. It was hard to hear her at first, since her face was pressed against her big sister's arm, but Ella understood. "You're forgiven." Then Lili looked up at her and added, "Will you forgive me for losing the book?"

"Yes, but it really wasn't your fault," Ella answered.

"I was just trying to help. I don't feel like I can do much." Lili paused before speaking again. "I'm afraid, Ella. What's going to happen to Mom now?" She stared at her sister with fear in her eyes.

Ella sat quietly, not sure what to say at first. She was fighting her own demons of doubt. "Well, I'm not sure, but I am sure that the sooner we find her, the sooner we can figure out what to do."

Ella pushed up from the damp ground and offered Lili a helping hand. "Ready to get going?"

"Yup," Lili said, grasping her hand and standing up. "Thanks."

"Thanks for forgiving me," Ella said with a quick hug. Lili hugged her back for a second, and Ella thought she heard her sister mumble something. "What was that?" she asked Lili.

"Oh nothing, just talking to myself. I was reminding myself of something mom told me yesterday. Don't worry about it. Let's go." Lili smiled weakly and grabbed her sister's hand as they walked back to Carey.

Carey was happy to see her sisters had worked out their problem. *That's one down, many more to go,* she thought. Mackay chose that moment to rejoin them. She seemed to have forgotten her anger at Ella. Now she was buzzing around the two sisters, smiling and burning like a happy yellow ball of light.

Lili was looking around, so Carey answered the question she saw in her eyes. "Alsoomse went to scout ahead. She thinks Aphina's camp isn't far away."

"What are we going to do, Carey?" Lili asked.

"For now, I'll scout around here and see what we have to work with. You guys stay here and wait for Alsoomse to return. While you're waiting, how about you check our supplies and stuff? You can see if we have anything that might be useful to fight Aphina with," Carey told her sisters. Then she added, "I sure hope you packed like I would've, Ella."

Carey picked up her spear. It felt a little more useful now that she had fought one battle with it. Nodding at her sisters, she walked off down the trail. She followed it to where the paths crossed, but where Alsoomse had turned right, she turned left. "I'll be right back," she called.

CHAPTER 15

Preparations

ALSOOMSE WAS THE FIRST TO RETURN. SHE had been right about Aphina's camp. She had found it, and it was just a few hills over. The animal tracks had turned into the woods right after the first rise, but Alsoomse assured them that they were not hard to follow in the forest. As she explained, the trees were close enough and tall enough that there was much less underbrush in this part of the woods.

Not long after Alsoomse's return, Carey got back, too. She made Alsoomse tell her part of the story again, then she told the girls about her trip. A river cutting straight through the park had stopped her from going too far, but Ella could tell from the look on her face that she seemed pleased with what she had found there. Ella always thought Carey looked like the Grinch on the cartoon special when she got that grin that crossed her face from ear to ear. Lili was curious. She tried to pry a few of the details from Carey, but all she would say was that they would have to wait until after they looked over Aphina's camp. "There's no point making plans without knowing what we're up against."

Getting near to the camp without making a bunch of noise was a lot harder for the girls than for Alsoomse. It seemed like every time one of them took a step they snapped a twig or crunched a dry leaf. Alsoomse was patient though, and with little bits of advice whispered to them from time to time, they were a bit quieter before they reached the camp. After what had seemed an eternity, they had finally reached where they were going. Alsoomse made Lili wait at the backside of a little rise while the rest of them went up the hill to investigate. They had made sure to advance with the wind in their faces, which had meant they had to go all the way around to the opposite side of the camp. Alsoomse said that this would make it impossible for the animals to pick out their scents. They had had to crawl the last bit, but now they were in position.

They were lying under some pine trees about twenty yards away from Aphina's hideout on a little knoll. The small prickly

pines above where they were lying formed a natural hedge across the tops of these little hillocks. Alsoomse told them that it provided the perfect place to spy on their enemies below. Each girl was lying on her stomach underneath the low hanging branches so she might look over the ridge without being seen. They watched for ten minutes without too much distraction, but as the minutes ticked by, it was getting harder and harder for Carey and Ella to ignore the ants that were crawling up and down their legs. Ella kept rubbing her legs together, while Carey bit her lip and tried not to scratch. It itched. It tickled. It seemed like the more they tried not to think about it, the more ants seemed to crawl all over them and get into their clothes. It was slow torture. The most frustrating part was that Alsoomse did not even seem to notice. Finally, Ella muttered to Carey, her eyebrows raised and jaw set, "Is she even human?"

It was hard, but their suffering was rewarded. After a short while they were fairly certain that their mother was not injured. She was tied up and sitting at the edge of the encampment. The small tree she was leaning against was one of many in the copse of trees that surrounded the campsite. As for Aphina, she was standing in front of a metal camping table. Her attention was fixed on the book. She kept flipping through pages and seemed to be talking to someone, though who she was talking to, the girls could not figure out. Carey and Ella burned with indignation. As they watched their mother suffering, their minds drummed with angry questions. *How could she treat our mother like some kind of wild animal? Who does she think she is? Why does she have to be so heartless?* At first these thoughts were like swatting at an annoying fly. It was hard to clear their minds, but as the frustration grew, so did the need to suppress their mounting fury. Taking hold of each other's hands, they squeezed them tightly. It was like clamping down on a bike brake when you feel like you're careening towards a ditch. They knew they had to stop themselves. As they held hands, they both closed their eyes and fought to think clearly. They had been taught all their lives to do their duty, and the thinking part of them knew their duty was not running down there and trying to rescue their mom without a plan, but the emotional part of them was making it really hard to listen to reason. It took great restraint, but as they fought back their tears and rage, they saw that the best thing they could do at that moment was plan. Being rash would not help anything.

"The camp's not too big. That should help," Ella whispered to the others.

"Yes, but we will have to draw the animals away. No good to

fight at enemies' village," said Alsoomse softly. "Their numbers are greater than ours. We will need a surprise."

"I agree," Carey said looking over the camp. She had that look on her face, the one she got whenever they used to play Knights and Princesses. She always liked to be the hero. "I count four coyotes, one badger, twelve foxes, and a shaggy dog that looks part wolf, or at least a hairy German shepherd, not to mention her crow and a few wounded owls."

"The rest of the birds must've flown away," Ella commented as they watched for a little bit longer.

"I can help you learn to fight, but we do not have much time for training. But I think the number is too great, even if I had long time to train you," Alsoomse said. She looked a little perplexed, her dark eyes intense, her thin black eyebrows pinched together as her forehead drew down with heavy thoughts.

"Hey Carey," exclaimed Ella, who spoke louder than she intended to. Before she could say anything else, Alsoomse placed her hand over her mouth, to remind her to lower her voice. After a few moments to make sure no one had overheard her, followed by another stern look, Alsoomse removed her hand. Ella whispered, "Remember what Mackay said back at South Island about Night Shade Dust?"

"A little," Carey answered, trying to recall the conversation while flicking yet another ant off her arm.

"She said that if Night Shade Dust gets wet, it washes off and stops working. What if we get the animals wet? They might start acting normal and then we would have a chance to frighten them away!"

"That's a good idea, Ella," Carey said.

"How are we to get them wet though?" Alsoomse asked.

"Well," Carey said, "I think I have an idea or two. Let's get to safer ground where we can talk it over and make some plans. I think we've seen all we are going to see up here."

The other girls nodded, then crawled down the hill backwards, trying to remain silent and unseen. Once they reached the middle of the hill where they could safely stand, they eased up and tip-toed the rest of the way down. Lili and Mackay met them at the bottom with eager faces. Mackay was popping like a white-hot sparkler with excitement. Lili tried to ask questions right away, but Alsoomse silenced her, and they headed to a safe place to plan.

Walking at a fast pace, it took a few long, silent minutes to reach the halfway point between the camp and the river. By then Lili was huffing and puffing and begging them to stop. The three older girls sat down on a fallen log, and Lili collapsed on the ground. Mackay, on the other hand, was so excited that she was burning like a hundred-watt light bulb. Once everyone had sipped a little water and caught their breath, the war council began. Carey cleared the ground in front of them with her foot and grabbed a stick to draw a map, but before she started sketching any plans, she asked a question: "What stuff did you guys grab?"

"Well, Lili and I packed lots of rope, a couple of raincoats, a blanket, our water bottles, some food, the camping tool kit, and our knives and spears."

"I wish we had some kind of gun, or at least your bow and arrows, Carey!" Lili added.

"Well we don't, but I think I have something that will work anyway," Carey said to encourage her little sister.

"What's that?" Ella asked, eager and impatient to know.

"Well, when I was looking around by the river, I found a place that the campers must have used for a swimming hole. There's a tire swing all rigged up. The path I followed goes right past the swing, which is right beside the river before the path turns up a hill." Carey explained all this as she drew a map in the dirt with her stick. "The river is on your left and the bank drops off into the water. The tire swing's old, but it looks safe enough. The kids must have loaded up the swing on the hill and swung out over the river and jumped in. It actually looks like a lot of fun, if it weren't for the big mess we're in."

"Okay, but how'll that help us?" Lili asked.

"Look," Carey said starting to draw her ideas in the dirt, "if we can get the animals to follow us up this trail here," she drew with the stick, "we could rig up a trap. See? Lili or someone could be waiting on the hill and when the animals follow us, she could swing down and knock them into the water."

"Yeah," Ella said catching on, "maybe we could even put a board or log across the tire and it would be like a battering ram or something like that."

"Great!" Carey said excitedly.

Alsoomse was silently weighing all the ideas, but Lili was eager to offer her own suggestions. "Maybe we can use the coats and dump water on them, too."

"That might work, Lili!" Carey said with enthusiasm as their plans took shape. "Alsoomse, can you make a trap for us? Something that Lili could somehow trigger on the hill? I don't know, maybe you could figure out how to use the raincoats and ropes or something like that?"

"I think I can try to do this thing," Alsoomse said, "but we will also need to practice with spears. It may be that some do not get wet, and we will have to fight."

Everyone nodded. Alsoomse had a good point. After they were agreed, they began to talk about specifics. In the middle of the planning Lili suddenly got quiet.

"What, Lili?" Carey asked, noticing her sister's stoic face. Mackay even stopped walking around the map and came over to pat Lili's leg.

"We forgot something," Lili's words trailed off into silence before fear squeezed the next words out: "What about Mom? What if Aphina hurts her?"

Their excitement was dampened by this new revelation. It *was* a possibility. One that they could not overlook.

"Well, then we'll have to get her out somehow," Ella finally answered, then added as an afterthought, "but how?"

Carey was rubbing her temples as she thought it all over, but then she stopped. As she looked up, she snapped her fingers, "What if we use some of us as bait? We will let ourselves be seen, something for the animals to attack. When they do, we could make sure all the animals follow us to the traps. Then Ella could sneak in and set Mom free during all the confusion."

"I want to help too," said Mackay, proudly volunteering.

"Sure, why not? You might even be able to find the pages that Aphina is hiding so we can send her back," Carey added.

"But what about Aphina?" Lili asked.

Preparations

Crestfallen, everyone plunged back into contemplation at Lili's important question. Each girl was racking her brain, hoping for an idea. Ella was chewing on the end of her braid, Carey was tapping the ground with her foot, and Lili was drumming on her chin with her fingertips. Suddenly Carey stopped tapping and her eyes grew hopeful and bright.

"Maybe some smoke will help. It'll make them all confused, and if we have enough Aphina might think it's a forest fire or something. It would make it hard for Aphina to see, so Ella could cut mom free and escape, while Mackay gets the pages."

There was a long silent pause as everyone thought the suggestion over. "It might work," Alsoomse said, "smoke would at least help to confuse the animals. It will make smelling hard."

"If it's decided then, let's get to work," Carey added with a nod.

Now that all the plans were made, Alsoomse and Ella stepped in to take command. They worked together to hand out orders for the jobs that needed to get done and everybody started working. Carey chuckled to herself. Did it really matter at this point who was in charge, as long as they rescued their mother?

After Ella and Carey had finished setting up the swing and Alsoomse had completed the water traps, the girls worked on the smoke screen. The piles had to be made just right if they were going to work. There would be three of them spread out behind a line of small hills near Aphina's camp. This part of their plan would take the longest to prepare. They were close enough to the camp that they could not afford being overheard. They also had to do the whole thing upwind, though Alsoomse had an idea to take care of that. Lili giggled as Alsoomse smeared who-knows-what on the girls' faces and arms. She was ticklish and did not seem to care what the stuff was. Carey and Ella, on the other hand, really did not want to know what it was, just as long as it helped to cover their scents.

"This will make us smell like forest," Alsoomse said.

Once the girls were covered with the goo, they set off. Little by little they collected the necessary sticks and branches from the surrounding forest and brought them to the spots appointed for them. They laid the wood in order, each one looking like a little teepee of sticks, then they placed dried leaves, shaved woodchips, and tiny twigs into the little alcoves underneath. The girls had had a lot of practice over the years in preparing a campfire, so Alsoomse was rather pleased when she inspected their handiwork.

The plan was to get the fires going so that they were sure they would not go out. Once they were strong, they would place layers of damp green leaves on top so that they smoked. They hoped it would look like their next-door neighbor's house in the fall. He always smoked everyone out when he burned his pile of leaves beside the road. Alsoomse had picked out the perfect spots, where the hills would hide the flames, but where the steady wind would still carry the smoke right down into the enemy's camp.

After preparing the farthest bonfire, Alsoomse walked up to Carey and Lili. They had almost finished their assignment. She inspected their work with her arms across her chest as they placed the remainder of their wet leaves near the stack of logs and sticks. Ella had been the first to finish her task and had headed back to the halfway point without waiting on Alsoomse. She had something she was going to talk over with Mackay. Once the girls placed their last handful of leaves on the pile, Alsoomse motioned for Carey and Lili to come with her. The look on her face indicated she had something to tell them. They were quite curious about what she wanted to say, but they had no choice but to follow her noiselessly. They would have to wait until they reached a safe place where they could talk and not be heard.

"Your little sister should not fight," Alsoomse declared, when they were almost to the halfway point. The way she said it and the stern set of her eyes told Carey that this was not a suggestion. The next moment her hard expression softened, and she spoke again, "If the plan works, I think she will not have to fight, but you, *you* might need to fight." She paused as if thinking over her words and at last added, "I watch you in the battle with the birds. You have passion, but you have no teaching. You must have both. Now, if you will let me, I will teach you things to help."

"All right, if you think you can," Carey said. She would try, but she was unsure as she took the spear offered her. It was sharp, very sharp. Alsoomse had been the one appointed to inspect their weapons during their preparations. Apparently, they had needed a little fine tuning. As she clutched the wood in her hand, the weight of it all hit her. She felt sick. She breathed deeply in and out a few times, then closed her eyes. Her hands were sweating, but there was no going back. Like her dad would say, "If you're thrown into the deep end, there's no better time to learn how to swim!" Alsoomse looked at her and waited. Carey nodded, and they began.

Alsoomse started by teaching her how to stand and hold the spear properly. Carey tried her best to pay close attention. There was nothing else for Lili to do, so she decided to sit on a nearby log and watch. "You need to spread your legs. If you stand with legs close, you will be easy to knock down. Always think balance. Bend, and you will not fall down. Be like a small tree that bends before a mighty wind. It is the hard, proud tree that falls in the storm," Alsoomse instructed. Step by step she showed her the proper and improper movements. Carey thought it all looked like a kind of dance as she moved in and out of each stance. At first, she only watched, then they stood side by side and Carey moved with her teacher. As she copied, Alsoomse corrected her. In the end Carey stood alone and went through the movements as Alsoomse watched. Carey was always quick to pick up sports or games, and it seemed that fighting was enough like dancing that she was going to catch on quickly. As the minutes ticked by, she moved through each step, dancing from form to form, between basic thrusts and blocks. As she began to tire, Alsoomse just waved at her to continue. Soon beads of sweat formed on her forehead and began to run down her face. Finally, she was given the signal to do it all one more time. This last time through she closed her eyes and tried to feel the movements. When she stepped out of the last form, she spun the spear around her extended fingers like a cheerleader with a baton. Then she stood up straight and tall and grinned from ear to ear.

She felt pretty satisfied with herself, but her head soon

deflated when Alsoomse looked at her without a smile and explained, "Now, all that I teach you is good against man, but we are not fighting man. Animal is different. Man is clever, but fears death. If animal is willing to attack man, he not fearing death. He has decided to kill. Blood is in his mind, and his only thought is *death-to-you*." Alsoomse was serious and stern and she stressed her last words by drawing them out as she spoke them to Carey.

"Okay," Carey said a little confused, waiting for her to explain.

"Your fear," Alsoomse said, "is your greatest enemy with animal. They want to attack from behind. They do not like to face a man's eye," she said pointing at her eyes with two outstretched fingers. "You must control your fear; stand your ground. It is like mighty buffalo when wolves attack: they stand and fight. You must not turn your back. You must not run away. To turn or to run is to die."

"If animal attack you," Alsoomse continued, "you stand like this." She stood alert, her legs spread apart with her spear pointing out in front of her in a threatening way. "Keep spear always between you and animal. You must hold it firm with two hands. Do not let one get behind you. If the animal jumps at you for short attack, stab like this." Alsoomse showed her a quick thrusting motion. "If you wound them, they may become tired and leave you, but they may become angry and fight more. They may seek to kill you fast."

Carey was nodding her head and trying to remember everything she was hearing. She went through the steps a few times while Alsoomse gave her time to think through her words.

Once she was satisfied with Carey's form, Alsoomse added her final instructions: "Just before animal attack, he will make noise and start to prepare. Then you must be ready yourself. When he crouches like this..." Alsoomse showed her by getting down on all fours and looking for all the world like a cat or dog that was about to lunge. She spoke to her from her position near the ground: "When you see this, you drop to one knee and hold out spear. You must rest end of spear in ground." When Carey looked at her blankly, Alsoomse hopped up and came over to show her what she meant. With spear in hand, she knelt down on one knee beside Carey. She showed her how to place the spear at a forty-five-degree angle and to place the butt of the weapon against her knee and the hard dirt as an anchor. After watching her, Carey tried, and Alsoomse corrected one or two small mistakes.

They were so intent on the training that they had both forgotten about Lili until she asked them a question: "Wow... will it really work?"

"It should, but do not drop spear," Alsoomse said to Carey with a hard, but good-natured slap to her shoulder.

"Ouch," Carey said, rubbing her shoulder and asking, "what happens if I drop the spear?"

"The animal is only wounded and you lose spear. Then again, he attacks, you die," she said without a hint of humor. Carey swallowed hard, and the two sisters looked at each other with wide eyes. During the moment of silence, Alsoomse stepped very close to Carey. She placed her strong hand on her shoulder and looked at her with intense walnut brown eyes. "You will not drop it. You will not fail, sister. Come." Turning, she walked away and motioned for Lili and Carey to follow.

After a short walk, the three girls met Ella at the planning ground. She and Mackay were sneaking around like they were playing a game of spy, and they had wiped more mud on their faces.

"What's that?" Lili asked, pointing at Ella's face.

"What this?" repeated Ella dramatically, while she and Mackay scrunched up their faces and showed their teeth. They hoped they looked dangerous. Then she added, "It's trolls' war paint."

Carey rolled her eyes. "Come on, enough playing around."

After checking all the weapons one last time and making

sure everyone had their knives and matches, they all stood there staring at each other. Alsoomse seemed to be the only one that was not shaking. Carey noticed Lili mumbling something and biting her lip.

"Are you okay, Lili?" she asked, bending over so that she could look her sister in the eyes.

"I'm just reminding myself of something Mom said to me yesterday."

After giving her sister a quick hug to reassure her, Carey said, "Lili, you'll be fine. Just do your job like we showed you." As she spoke, she counted off the tasks on her outstretched fingers. "Remember the steps: you pull the rope when the animals are under the coats, then you jump on the swing and hit the animals. After the swing goes back up, you hold onto the tree, and last, you stay hidden on the hill until we call you. Got it?" As her big sister recited each task Lili thought she sounded an awful lot like her mother.

"Got it," Lili said, running each thing over in her mind so she would not forget anything.

"Next time we meet, we'll have Mom," said Carey, and then she added, "so don't worry."

After a few parting hugs between the sisters, Lili ran to her post.

"We must go," Alsoomse said, as the girls watched their little sister leave.

Carey clinched her spear. "Okay, ready or not, here we come," she said as the three girls trotted off to the fire pits.

CHAPTER 16

It Begins

AREY WIPED HER SWEATY PALMS ON HER shirt. *Why does it have to be so quiet?* she thought. It was as if the whole forest had been turned off: no birds, no animals, not even a rustle of leaves, just silence. The stillness made time stretch out like those nervous moments before a final exam. Carey felt numb. She'd decided that her desire to live out the adventures in books was overrated. Quietly she approached her fire pit. Fumbling, she pulled out her matches. Her hands were shaking so badly she was sure the animals below could hear every last match rattling around in the little cardboard box. But she was determined. They had to finish this and save her mom.

She watched as Alsoomse gave the designated signal, a

swift chop of her raised hand. Carey then waved the signal to Ella who was waiting on the far side. That is when she noticed Mackay hovering just above Ella's shoulder. They had both wiped their war paint from off their faces, but Mackay must have found some wild berries. With the juice of these, she had replaced her mud with blue handprints on her arms and shoulders and had placed swirls and patterns on her neck and face. If she had not been so cute, she would have looked quite terrifying. She even had a limb from a thorn bush as a weapon. She could tell Mackay was excited, as she was having a hard time trying to dim her fairy fire. It made her look like a Christmas light with a short in it. Her light was blinking white, then blue, then yellow, switching every few seconds when she lost control and let it shine out.

Time suddenly regained its momentum as Carey tried to start her fire, her nervous mind checking off the points of the plan in rapid succession. She struck match after match, before one caught the dry leaves. She had to help the little tongues of fire with a few soft puffs of breath before the stack was burning with a strong steady flame. Then she looked up the line both ways and noticed each fire was burning. Alsoomse was crouched over her fire but was watching all three attentively. When she judged the flames to be strong enough, she gave the next signal, which meant that they were to place the wet leaves on top.

Carey sprinkled the leaves carefully so as not to put the fire out, just like Alsoomse had taught her. Handful by handful, she methodically layered the green leaves until they covered the whole fire. As she waited, the leaves began to sizzle ever so slightly, and soon tendrils of smoke were snaking out through the cracks between the leaves. Within moments, heavy smoke was pouring out. It choked the air and grew into an ever-increasing cloud. The wind blew in a steady steam over their shoulders and into the camp below and with it, the heavy acrid smoke.

With a thumbs-up to her younger sister, who was now crouched on the backside of the hill, Carey headed over to where Alsoomse was going to meet her. Ella smiled back and waved as she and Mackay moved to the rear of Aphina's camp where they would wait until they saw the opportunity they needed to free their mother.

"We wait down there. It is clear of smoke, and we will not be surprised," Alsoomse whispered, as Carey reached her side. She was pointing down the trail just a short way to where there were fewer trees and bushes.

Carey muffled a cough and then whispered, "Let's go." The smoke was everywhere now, and she was forced to wave it away from her face. Blinking back tears, she followed Alsoomse as they hurried down the hill, leaving the billowing smoke behind them.

"You will tell me how this infernal book works," demanded Aphina, turning in frustration from the book. It was laid open on her table, but it was not yielding its secrets as she had hoped. Her intense purple eyes bore into Patty, "How do I unlock the magic it holds?"

Aphina had been reading the book ever since her crow and two owls had returned. The others had not come back. Though they had managed to steal the book, the fact that many of Aphina's minions appeared to be dead made Patty feel a little bit better. She thought, *at least the girls put up some kind of a fight*. Aphina had barely noticed her slaves' reduced numbers. She had even shushed her crow's reports once she greedily held the book. She read and re-read the book immediately. From the very first, her expressions had betrayed her. She had been shocked that the book contained children's tales, though as quickly as the shock had covered her face, it had been replaced by obstinance. Muttering oaths under her breath, she had refused to believe what she saw—that in fact, the book was simply a collection of fairy stories. Though hours had passed, she was no closer to unlocking the book's meaning, so her suspicious mind told her that the book must be coded. There must be a secret that kept the power of the book hidden. When this thought seized her, she became obsessed.

She tried every pattern and combination that she could think of, but ended up with page after page of meaningless notes and senseless gibberish. Eventually, for the briefest of moments, she thought she might have unlocked the code, but despite all her hard work, she was still unable to figure it out. That was when Aphina decided to read it aloud. Patty had gotten quite nervous at that point, but for some reason it did not work for her. She could only assume it must not work for characters that were a part of the book itself. When reading aloud did not work, Aphina began raving and mumbling under her breath. She tried reading every other word, then only the first words of every paragraph, and then the last words of every page. She paced like a caged lion. With a glowering face she drummed the table with her fingers and tapped the ground with her foot. She pressed on, heedless of the nonsensicalness of it all. She would not, could not, stop her efforts to unlock this book's power. She turned around in total frustration.

She straightened a lock of her hair that had fallen out of place and calmed her breathing, then she approached Patty. Though her face was now demure and smooth like a china doll's and the flush in her cheeks gone from sight, her eyes still boiled with fury. She spoke, "You will confess, mother dearest. Sooner or later, you will!" Her vow was made with a cool empty smile that made Patty cringe despite her efforts not to.

The breeze carried the scent of burning leaves and the clearing gradually filled with smoke. They both looked about to find its source. Patty noticed that the wooded hills surrounding the camp were filled with clouds of smoke. They made the tall trees standing about look like a congregation of specters, their long, crooked arms reaching out like ghosts in a wall of gray smoke that descended into the camp.

The animals began to cough and sneeze. Aphina waved a hand in front of her face and plugged her nose. *Was it a forest fire?* Patty wondered, *could I be that lucky?*

"Byrne," Aphina commanded through the dense smoke. It was now rolling in like morning fog off a lake, obscuring the harsh light of the afternoon sun. Even sitting on the ground, Patty's lungs burned with the acrid fumes. The tears in her red, irritated eyes made it hard to focus. She had no way to protect herself from the offending cloud that filled her eyes, nose, and throat, as her hands were tied behind her back, but in spite of this, something inside her sprang up hopefully at this unexpected turn of events. She stubbornly kept her eyes open. Doing so, she noticed that Aphina's eyes were also red and irritated. With a scowl, Aphina turned and barked a command at her underling. "Take the owls and see what this cursed smoke is all about. Something does not smell right."

Byrne cawed like a creaky old door in a dusty, abandoned house, then the crow and the remaining two owls filled the ashen air with the flapping of their wings as they launched from their perches. All the other animals were milling about now, trying to find a place below the fumes. They seemed restless and Patty figured that the Night Shade Dust was the only thing that was keeping them from obeying their natural instincts to run. As for Aphina, who now appeared only as a vague outline in the ever-increasing bleakness, she just covered her nose with a perfumed handkerchief and walked away. She coughed just once through the smoke as she spoke to Patty, "I will deal with you in a moment, mother dearest."

Carey and Alsoomse heard the birds before they saw them. They were cawing and hooting, and then they suddenly burst through the smoke like three cannon balls. The girls were ready, but the birds were not. They had not thought to find their enemies standing ready to meet them on the level ground just beyond the gray smoke wall that surrounded their camp. The ambush took them totally by surprise. Startled squawks and muffled hoots slipped from their open beaks as they tried to adjust their flight paths.

In a blur, Alsoomse spun her spear like a quarter staff, striking the two owls to the ground before they could escape. Byrne, who was always looking for an advantage, had chosen the weaker target, and cawed in rage as he swooped down. His hope was to peck at Carey's eyes. The crow's overconfidence was his mistake, for he did not know of Alsoomse's training, and was unaware that this time Carey was more prepared. She waited as the crow approached her, her feet planted firmly on the ground. This time she watched her attacker, like a batter watches a baseball. There would be no blind swinging. Her mind screamed, *swing!* as she gripped the wood like a bat and swung at the crow's diving body. Though she hit a little off center, the spear pierced the crow's right wing and breast.

Stunned, the crow jerked away in pain, whirling about on

a sudden gust of wind. Alsoomse turned, trying to knock the beast out of the air like a child swinging at a swaying piñata. The bird was now beyond their reach. Circling with difficulty, the crow turned for home, carried on the wind with feeble outstretched wings. His cawing filled the empty forest with his injured cries.

"He got away," Carey said in frustration.

"Do not be troubled. I think he will help the plan," Alsoomse said, placing a hand on Carey's shoulder. "Soon they will come. You go to river. I will meet you there," she commanded.

"No," Carey protested, but Alsoomse cut her off with a raised hand and a stern look.

"You are slower than me, sister, go before me," she said as she grabbed her arm and took a few steps with her down the path as she spoke again, "I will not fight them here, but someone must be prey. I will join soon."

Carey did not like it, but she gave a reluctant nod of her head. She gripped her spear and spoke quietly but firmly, "I'll be waiting." Then she bolted from the clearing like a startled doe and followed the trail to the river.

Ella was close now. At least, she felt very certain that she was close. She could not see where she was going at this point and was guided solely by memory and instinct. The dense smoke had covered her movements as planned, but it also made it hard to maneuver. At first, moving around in it had not been her greatest concern. The girls loved playing hide and seek in the dark, so she had a well-developed sense of direction even when she was unable to see. Her greatest concern had been how to breathe. She tried her best not to cough. She worried it would give her location away. Smoke might blind eyes and cover scents, but it could not make animals or people deaf. Fortunately, before she had reached the first set of trees, she had remembered something from a book she had read. She hoped it would help. Hiding behind a large bush, she had stopped to douse her handkerchief with water from her canteen and had wrapped it around her face. Mackay had laughed at that, her giggles sounding like a twittering little bird. She had flown right beside her, trying not to blink yellow fairy fire, and had whispered in Ella's ear. She had told her that the Southland women on the coast covered their faces when they were looking to marry. Ella had waved her away and tried not to blush. After she had covered her nose and mouth, she had only to find her way. That had taken a little longer than she had hoped, but now she was quite certain that she was near the camp. The fumes were oppressive, and the smoke fought to enter her lungs and obscure anything that was more than a few inches above the ground, but if she was right, her mother was just a few feet away.

Now began the waiting game. She wet her handkerchief one more time for good measure, then she left her backpack and water bottle behind a nearby tree. Using an army crawl, she advanced as quietly as she could until she lay on the backside of a little bluff. The grass tickled her chin as she listened and waited for the right moment to move forward. Ella tried to control her breathing, which came in sporadic puffs. She exhaled and inhaled slowly, calming the raging emotions and thoughts that beat against her common sense. She felt blind in all this gray smog, but just as a blind man's hearing improves because of a lack of sight, so did Ella's. As she lay there, she began to pick out movements from the camp. This helped to improve her awareness, but not her anxiety.

"Mackay," Ella said, taking a chance and whispering ever so quietly to her friend, "I can't see a thing, but I doubt that Aphina has left the stolen pages out in the open. Go over to where the cave is and check around there," she instructed. Mackay flitted away with a smile on her face. Then more to herself than to the fairy she added, "But please don't get caught!"

After Mackay disappeared into gray nothing, Ella looked in front of her again. She could not really see anything, but being this close to the ground at least helped her see the little that could be seen. It sounded as if the animals were still around. She could hear the dog and coyotes whimpering at their master. They seemed to be farther away than before, closer to the hills on the other side of the camp. Though she strained her ears, she could not hear anything that sounded like Aphina. As she listened, she suddenly heard a slight cough. It came from the tree right in front of her on the opposite side of the bluff. Without thinking, she pressed herself to the ground, fearing lest someone should somehow see her. That is when she saw what was just a few feet in front of her. Her heart leaped in her breast when she realized it was her mother. She recognized the hands that were tied together at the back of the tree. She had not gotten lost after all. In fact, she realized she could almost reach out and touch those precious hands. It took all her willpower to suppress the sudden impulse, but she managed it with difficulty. Now that she was certain where she was, she crossed her fingers and hoped. All she needed was the right moment to free her mother.

Byrne came lurching through the smoke, cawing with a strange painful cry—one that Aphina had never heard him use before. He collapsed on her outstretched arm as he landed. He was bleeding from a wound in his breast and wing.

"Byrne, what happened?" Aphina asked. She spoke harder than she intended to because her fear had curdled her concerns into anger.

The wounded crow blinked his black eyes once or twice before he gave one or two half-hearted caws, which sounded more like the muffled croaks of a frog in a boy's pocket than anything close to his normal way of speaking. Steadying the wounded bird with one of her hands, Aphina took him over to the table. Though it grated on her nerves, she disrupted her organized table by hastily pushing all the items to the side in an irritating jumble of confusion. She laid her patient on this cleared off space with more gentleness then you might expect, my reader. For one moment she almost looked like a concerned mother hovering over a sick child, then it was gone. With her cold, scientific mind enthroned once more, she deftly assessed Byrne's wounds, noting all his injuries and listening to his report.

"Those little children did this?" Aphina asked, raising her

voice to an almost shrill pitch of rage and shock. She really did believe what she had said earlier about love making a person weak. She had forgotten its power. With eyes bulging and veins pulsing in her temples, Aphina turned from her wounded servant. With a sharp clap of her hands, she summoned the other animals who whimpered and milled around, confused by all the smoke.

"Forest creatures, come!" she commanded, her eyes wide with zealous intensity. Within moments, the groups of animals had formed ranks, each according to its species. She walked in front of them, like a general inspecting an army. "Go to the woods," she said her voice rising into the bleak sky above, "and bring back these impudent children. Do not kill them, but drag them back here, crying and screaming for mercy."

With a wave of her hand, and a shudder in Patty's heart, Aphina turned. The animals scurried into the woods as she busied herself with the task of saving her pet's life. Aphina muttered to herself, but Patty could not make out her words. The slender woman stood over the crow like a surgeon standing over a patient. Her hands seemed to fly back and forth, using the tools she had, grabbing different jars from off the table, and retrieving items from her satchel, but Patty had to imagine most of these details. In the growing smoke she could see less and less all the time.

Aphina applied all her skills, but she knew that the resources in her camp were quite limited. Her anger boiled over. Despite her efforts, she realized that all her attempts to save her bird's life would be in vain. Patty watched the princess press her hand down on the table as if to steady herself, but then Aphina shook her head like a stubborn man that refuses to accept the obvious. The last thing she saw was the defiant look in Aphina's eyes as the smoke enveloped her and hid her from Patty's sight. She could not cover her nose, but she could close her eyes, and as she did, she prayed a little prayer for her children's safety.

Mackay's gotta be at the cave by now, Ella figured. Then she heard Aphina cry out in rage. *Great!* she thought to herself, *the plan's moving along. Now, I've just got to wait for my part.* Not long after that Ella heard Aphina bellow a command, "Go to the woods." Those words worked like a signal flag in all that gray gloom. She knew it was now or never. This would be her one and only chance to set her mother free. Swallowing hard and taking a deep breath, she stuck her hand out over that little rise. Ever so carefully she moved forward over the ground. She was trying so hard not to make any noise that she realized she was holding her breath. She was grateful for her earlier glimpse of her mother. It comforted her to know that she only had a few feet to go. It would have been very easy to get lost in all this smoke, like a confused child attempting to pin the tail on the donkey after being spun around too much. Then a sudden doubt attacked her mind. *What if you're going the wrong way?* said the unwanted voice. Ella was not one given to much doubting, but she shuddered before she could push away this disturbing thought. She reached for the hand that she hoped was hidden in the gloom. As she did, she thought, *I sure hope Mackay has found the missing pages.*

The passing minutes felt more like years to Mackay. Once she left Ella, she could not trust herself to fly in all the dense smoke, so she walked. She hummed a nervous little tune as she went along, looking more like a child playing soldier than the brave warrior she wanted to be. She scurried between large stones, squatted behind toadstools, ran beside a fallen log, and inched along as best she could. The journey progressed slowly, and the delay was hard for her to accept. Fairies are not naturally patient people, so she could not comprehend the fact that some things just take time. Halfway through her journey the pace became unbearable, so she began to fly in short bursts, much like a grasshopper jumping between tall blades of grass. She watched after each landing, hoping she was not seen, and then scouted for the next place she would go. It was not easy in all that creepy smoke. All along she struggled with her fairy fire. It was so hard not to shine. Her emotions were burning inside her like the core of a tiny little sun. They always seemed to be boiling and rolling within her. They constantly fought to escape in eruptions of passionate color. It felt a lot like it does when you try to hold your breath for a really long time. Sooner or later all you can do is think about breathing, and then it gets very hard not to. She just wanted to let it burn. At that particular moment, her feelings had changed to fear, and she was fighting back the blue flames trying to escape from every pore of her skin. Fortunately for her, she had reached the end of her journey. She had made it through the trees that lined the back of the camp and had discovered the cave entrance on the far side. Her blue feelings of fear shifted, and her insides filled with the warm sensations of excitement and satisfaction. Her feelings were beguiling, but she was determined. She would not let the white-hot flames out, no matter how hard they pressed against her.

Now she pinched her lips together. She stretched her neck out from behind a blade of grass, while she held her thorny twig like a club. Her forehead crinkled and her eyes squinted as she searched the cave entrance for snakes or any other dangerous animals. "By the Fairy King's pointy shoe... I hate snakes," Mackay said to herself with a shudder. Then she closed her eyes and exhaled slowly. She needed to calm her beating heart. She was fairly certain the coast was clear. *It's now or never. Are you a fairy warrior or a scared little mouse?* Mackay asked herself. The truth was that she felt like a mouse, but she knew her new friends needed her help. Suddenly the words of her father came rushing back to her. It was almost like she could her him speaking them again, though he had been dead for many years. "Little one, remember, emotions are good servants, but bad masters. Even a fairy must do her duty." The words stoked the white flames burning inside her, but she suppressed them. She knew what she must do. Tentatively, like a child placing her toes into a lake so as to test the water before jumping in, Mackay stuck out her foot from behind the tuft of grass that hid her. *Here it goes. Please, oh please, don't let there be any snakes,* Mackay thought. She knew it would be just like Aphina to have a nasty little surprise like that waiting. Luckily for her, Aphina had been too busy with the book to find any. Nothing slithered, nothing barked, nothing moved, so she came out of her hiding place. It took her only about twenty fast steps to reach the cave's entrance, but they felt like an eternity to her. Without looking inside, she rounded the corner and went in.

Upon entering, she discovered that the cave was rather bare. There was a makeshift pillow, a rug to sleep on, a few candles, and some odds and ends. "Well, well, well, we have fallen a great distance from our mighty castle, haven't we? Humph!" said Mackay smuggly. She began flittering around, curiously stopping to look at everything while trying to locate Aphina's satchel. After rummaging through what was on the ground, she spotted a bleached deer skull sitting on a rock shelf at the other end of the cave.

"That *would* be the type of place Aphina would hide something," Mackay said to herself. She allowed her body to burn with a golden yellow fire. Joy was, after all, always the hardest emotion for her to control. *I'm inside. No one can see me,* she thought. As all the little flames crackled along the surface of her skin, she sighed and closed her eyes. She let herself revel a little in her emotional freedom. It was a lot like letting yourself enjoying a double-scooped ice cream cone on a really hot summer's day.

Making sure not to pass in front of the open doorway, Mackay flitted over to the shelf and landed on the rock ledge. The deer skull was looking at her with hollow eyes. As those empty sockets stared at her, Mackay's fairy fire turned to a deep blue. "Stop it, Mackay," she told herself in a serious voice, trying to work up her courage. She placed her hands on her hips and shook her head. Scolding herself she said, "Don't be a foundling, it's just a skull. It won't hurt you."

She took a few cautious steps closer. Once she reached those bleached bones, she bent over to peer through the eye hole. As she looked inside, the skull took on a strange blue hue, reflecting the glow of her fairy fire. She was unable to see anything from outside, so she would have to take a look inside. She held the cool boney rim with both hands then winced as she stuck her head all the way inside the hole. She felt queasy and her stomach rolled. It reminded her of a time she had watched a traveling entertainer at a mid-winter festival back home. He had wrestled with a dancing bear. Once or twice he had even put his head into its gaping mouth. She was certain that he was crazy, and now here she was doing almost the same thing. With effort she pushed the memory away and opened her eyes.

Right in front of her was a stack of parchments—parchments someone had cut out of a book.

"I've found it!" Mackay quietly exclaimed as she removed her head from the eye hole. Now her whole body radiated with bright yellow light.

CHAPTER 17

The Battle

AREY COULD HEAR THE ANIMALS CALLING to each other. Their barks, yips, and growls formed a confusing conversation that echoed through the canopy of trees. She was stepping from foot to foot in a nervous little dance. Her excitement made it impossible to stand still. Her stomach was aflutter. The next moment Alsoomse came careening around a bend in the path. She was signaling to Carey with her free hand. "Run! They are not far behind," she shouted, urging Carey to hurry before she caught up to her.

Carey heard the excited cries of the coyotes as they found their scent and called out, but she had no idea who led the pack. Most of these animals were working against their natural instincts by hunting with each other, but the Night Shade Dust forced them into obedience. The surrounding woods were filled with a chorus of discordant sounds. It made the hair on her arms stand on end. She felt more like a hunted rabbit than a brave hero. She had to stop thinking about that though. What she needed to do was concentrate on getting to the river before that pack caught up to her.

Rounding a last bend, they saw the river just a few yards away. Carey's lungs were burning, and she had a serious ache in her side, but the relentless pace of Alsoomse beside her—not to mention the sound of the wild animals behind her—kept her moving.

Following the trail to their destination, they crested a low rise and burst through two big bushes. These narrowed the path that emptied into the clearing. Hope filled Carey's heart as she heard the rippling river just a few steps in front of them. They would have just enough time to turn and catch a few breaths before the first ranks of the pack came tumbling through the underbrush.

The twelve foxes came first. With heaving sides and panting tongues, they stepped into the open. They slipped through the crease in the hedge and formed a half circle. Turning down their ears and smiling slyly with their wicked little fangs, they approached their prey. They crouched as they came and growled low in their throats, but before they had taken even two steps forward, the badger came rumbling along. His gray nose was sniffing at the ground. His aged eyes were filled with what appeared to be anger at being forced to rise before he had finished his nap. The foxes parted to make room for this newcomer. As he stepped forward, he let out a long hiss followed by a deep, rumbling growl.

The plan was to try and look afraid. Alsoomse tried her best, but she was not too convincing. Carey, on the other hand, was much more convincing, because she was actually terrified. Once the animals were certain the girls were cornered, they advanced ever so slowly. The girls lowered their spears. Carey willed her eyes to look at the animals. She must not look at the raincoats hanging right above them. As she stood there waiting, she hoped that none of the water would leak out and give away their little surprise. For a few drawn-out moments they were at a stand-still: bared teeth and bared spears. Though the cries from the wolf and coyotes sounded closer all the time, the badger and the foxes would not wait. The instincts of the hunt were too strong, so they impatiently pressed forward.

Suddenly Carey raised her arm and gave a jerking

hand-signal to her sister who was sitting up on the hill and screamed, "Now!"

Lili yanked the rope with all her might and the taut cords tipped the bulging rain coats over. The trap sent a shower of rushing water down on the unsuspecting animals. The foxes and badger sang out in a surprised chorus of yips and yowls. Their whole bodies were doused in the downpour and the Night Shade Dust ran off their coats in sparkling rivulets.

Carey turned and tried to give Alsoomse a high-five, but the other girl just looked at her with eyebrows raised and forehead crinkled with confusion. Just then the first coyotes parted the underbrush. Carey slowly raised her hand to give her little sister the next signal. She hesitated, waiting for the rest of the pack to join them. There was no need to rush since the first two coyotes were tangled in a snarling mass of angry animals. The foxes and badger were whimpering and biting at each other while the coyotes tried pushing their way through the melee. Everything was going according to plan until Carey's hand reached the height of her shoulder. That was when Lili misunderstood. She thought Carey's raised hand was the signal to launch her swing, so she did. Carey watched in horror as Lili let go of the branch she was holding onto and came barreling down on the group of shocked enemies below.

Lili's brown eyes were wild with excitement, and she bellowed the word "Attack!" With each passing second the tire-swing increased its velocity. The addition of the heavy log braced between the rope holding the tire added momentum as it careened down the hill. The animal noises stopped instantly, and each set of eyes grew to twice their normal size as the pack watched this demon beast come flying down upon them. The two foxes closest to the front tried to escape, but the sudden terror that seized the animals only added to the overall confusion. Claws scratched on the hard-packed dirt, creatures shoved at each other, but nothing helped. Before even one of the animals in the swarming mass could move, the log crashed into them. Carey and Alsoomse ducked and watched as Lili and the tire-swing made an absolutely fabulous disaster of their enemies. The next moment, animals were flying through the air. Creatures flew every which way. It looked as if someone had blown up a taxidermy shop.

The river's surface was pelted with clusters of furry bodies. The surrounding trees echoed the *splunk, splash, splunk* as the animals hit the water. Before the pack managed to come up for air, they were free from the spell that had possessed them. The drenched badger, the dazed foxes, and the confused coyotes paddled to the shore with all their might, while the Night

Shade dust floated down river. Now that their instincts were back in control, there was only one thought in their minds: to get far away from the *evil bird* that had swung down on them from the sky.

Lili was swinging backwards up the hill, when the last three animals burst through the bushes, and there was nothing she could do about it. That is, after all, how swings work, my reader. When she realized what had happened, she shuddered. The traps were all sprung. There was nothing to block their path now. Besides that, even if she made a fresh attack with her tire swing, they were out of reach where they now stood in the clearing.

At first, they stood smirking, their tongues hanging out of their mouths panting. Then they tensed and leered. The two coyotes and the large stray wolf-dog stood with bared teeth. As their throats rumbled, strands of saliva dripped from their curled black lips.

Ella had finally found her mother, but she was not yet free. Her shaking hands fumbled to find the rope that tied her to the tree. Once she found the knot, she squeezed her mother's soft hands with her trembling fingers. This startled Patty. She was not sure what had touched her, but she began swatting at whatever it was. Her first thought was that it was overly curious squirrel. As Patty swatted at her, Ella reached around the tree and covered her mother's mouth. Knowing her mother, she hoped she would not get bitten. As the hand appeared out of the smoke and covered her mouth, Patty managed one muffled gasp, then Ella pulled herself up and whispered into her mother's ear, "It's me, Ella! Stop making noise!"

Ella hoped Aphina had not heard. There was no way of knowing anything for sure in that heavy smoke, though it now seemed to be thinning out ever so slightly. As this thought hit her so did the realization that she would have to work fast.

She hunkered back down behind the tree, trying to stay hidden as she fished her knife out of her pocket. It was tangled in the folds. She tried to listen as she worked. It is strange how pockets seem to lose what you want them to keep and hold on to what you want them to let go of. Finally, after what seemed like an eternity, she got it out. She pulled out the blade ever so carefully. She knew it would click with a metallic pop if she did it too fast. Once it was open, she whispered into her mother's ear from the other side of the tree, "Stay still and act normal. I am going to cut you free."

The ropes were strong cords, much thicker than she had

planned. Besides that, it was much harder to cut them because of the way they were tied around her mother's wrists. Each second pulsed in her ears as her heart thudded in her chest and her palms began to sweat. She was becoming concerned that she would be seen in the thinning smoke, so Ella laid back down on the grass. There was nothing else for her to do but to lay on her back with her hands straight up in the air. It was the only way she could keep cutting without the risk of being seen. This position was safer, but much harder to work from. Ever so often she had to stop to let her arms rest and let the blood flow back into her fingers. Everything was taking too long. They had not planned for thick ropes. Ella had to crush the cry of frustration that wanted to burst from her lips. After sawing and sawing at the rope, wasting too many precious moments, Ella had cut most of the way through the first rope and part way through the second. It was beginning to fray where she was cutting it. Ella stopped to rest her hands for what she hoped was the last time and looked around for Mackay. *Where is she?* she thought. The smoke was so thin. It was more like a mist now than a dense fog. They needed to get away as soon as possible. Then she noticed that everything around her seemed eerily quiet. Panicked, Ella redoubled her efforts. Her knife slipped in her sweaty palm as she hacked at the bonds with all her strength. Her thoughts were screaming in her ears—*cut, cut, cut, cut*. Then a foreboding feeling seized her. She shivered and goose bumps rose on her arms, her worries multiplied in the stillness that surrounded her. *Where is Aphina?* she wondered. Suddenly, long powerful fingers pressed down on Ella's shoulder. A strong hand grabbed Ella's wrist and her whole hand tingled with the pain. There was no way to cut her mother's ropes now. The hand pulled her back without effort, though she was struggling with all her might, and she heard a smooth satiny voice say, "Well, what have I got here?"

"Ella, run!" Patty screamed, but it was too late. Aphina had her.

"Let go of me!" Ella yelled as she was lifted off the ground. In midair she was left dangling by her arms, kicking furiously, like an angry cat. Ella struggled. *How could such a slight woman be so strong?* Those hands gripped her like iron shackles. They never budged as she fought to get free. She kicked. She writhed. She squirmed. She was desperate. She knew she must get free, even if it meant using her knife. She tried everything she could think of while she screamed and hollered, but no matter what she did, nothing helped. She hung there like a trussed-up turkey waiting to be slaughtered.

"Let go of me!" Ella screamed. In one last burst of frustration she tried to kick Aphina as hard as she could, but she only kicked the air. Aphina shook her for that, rattling the teeth in her head.

"Stop fighting, young one. I have you, and your precious family *will* join you soon enough," Aphina mocked with a grin. With her free hand she knocked the knife away. Ella's hopes fell as she watched her knife land point first in the ground a few feet from her mother. She hung there limply, staring at the knife, fighting back tears.

Aphina lowered Ella and wrenched her arm behind her back. Now that she had her full attention, she dragged her away from her mother. Ella stopped all her protests as hot pain shot up her twisted arm. Her tormentor knew what she was doing. She had not broken her arm, but she was making it as painful as Ella could bear. As she tied her up, Aphina hissed into her ear through perfect white teeth, "Stop fighting, girl. There is no more hope."

Carey fought to control herself. Her erratic emotions pulled at her to run away and hide, while her brain repeated the training that Alsoomse had given her. She could hear the stern but stoic voice saying, "Your fear must be controlled, sister."

She noticed then that Alsoomse was already fighting two coyotes. They were working together. She was wheeling around in tight circles, keeping step with their movements while thrusting her spear at them with quick little jabs. The coyotes snapped at the stick with increasing irritation. Their jaws were foaming as if they were rabid. The seconds ticked by as they tested her defenses. One had already learned not to underestimate its prey. It had received a deep gash on its face as payment when it had tried to hamstring her. They were learning from their mistakes though, and now they were working as a group. Each coyote sought to attack from an opposite side, and Alsoomse was having to watch both directions at once. Carey could see the sweat beading on her forehead which made her face shine. As the coyotes lunged and growled, Alsoomse began swinging her spear in arcs and circles. The wood whistled as it cut through the air in a deadly dance. The battle was taking too long, and soon they stopped their excited yipping and became silent with intense rage. They were both watching for the same opportunity. If Alsoomse let down her guard for just a moment, one would attack her from behind.

Carey focused her thoughts on the task before her. This

was not the time for daydreaming. The wolf-dog before her was a mess. Its long shaggy hair was dirty and matted, and its ribs were sticking out. It was stepping back and forth as if pacing behind an invisible fence. It was barking but not growling. After one or two steps back and forth it would suddenly lunge forward a step, but then it would fall back as if it was uncertain of what to do next. The dog-half seemed at war with the wolf-half, though the Night Shade Dust appeared to be tipping the balances. Something inside told her it would not be long now. When that thought registered, she took a few precious moments to wipe her sweating palms on her shirt tail and take a firm grip on her spear.

Two or three seconds ticked by and then the Night Shade Dust crushed all resistance. Abruptly it stopped shuffling and stood still. It crouched, bringing its body close to the ground. The hair on the nape of its neck stood straight up. The barking stopped as the hair climbed to its full height and an angry growl rumbled in its throat. The noise rolled up and out again and again, like the sounds of an approaching thunderstorm. Immediately everything that might have been friendly disappeared, and it was replaced by a foaming zealot of its former self. Its eyes were aflame now with pure hatred, and a tendril of saliva hung from the corner of its mouth.

The first thing it tried was to bite Carey's right leg, the one she was leading with, but dogs do not do much hunting for their livings, so its slower reflexes earned it a quick jab in the shoulder. As the spear drew blood, the wolf-dog gave a sharp piercing yelp of pain and jerked back. That provided her some time as it thought over its next move. In those moments the wolf-half pulled from its forgotten storehouse of instincts the accumulated wisdom of its wilder ancestors, and with them it made its choice. It stopped and slowly crouched. The growling stopped. It knew now that it must go for the throat. In this new disturbing silence, Carey heard the sharp cry of one of the coyotes as it died.

It was now a pure beast. Its eyes leered as the scent of blood filled its nostrils. The smell of the dying coyote drove it to the brink of insanity. It crouched so low it almost lay on the ground, and its legs were like tensed, coiled springs. When the hairs on its stomach brushed the ground, its body froze for an instant. It was waiting for the right time to release its fury on her, and Carey knew her moment had come. As it leaped, she dropped to one knee and planted her spear against her kneecap and the ground. All she could do now was hold on for dear life and hope it would work.

The wolf was already leaping when she dropped to her

defensive stance. Eyes closed, Carey felt the weight of the animal slam into the tip of her spear. She struggled to keep the swinging paws at a safe distance with her weapon. Now she knew why Alsoomse had insisted on making a new longer one. The wolf howled in pain. Its mournful wails distracted the last coyote, and Alsoomse used it to her advantage. She stabbed it deftly, pinning the beast to the ground. Both animals fought and cried. They pawed the ground with frightening strength as they died. And then it was over. When Carey's spear stopped moving, she dared to open her eyes. Now that it was safe, her shaking hands dropped the weapon which was sticking out of the lifeless animal. It was the middle of summer, but she felt cold all over and shivered, while her blonde hair was damp and clinging to her face. Grabbing a handkerchief from her back pocket she wiped away the sweat and tears that stung her eyes. Then she inspected the scratches on her forearms and hands. She would live. Alsoomse limped over, nursing a serious cut on her leg. Carey mechanically ripped two strips of cloth from her shirt. Using a trick she had seen in a movie, she hoped she could staunch their bleeding wounds. She handed one strip to Alsoomse, who was not interested in having a nurse maid, and used the other on her arm. Without warning, relief, fear, pain, and disgust came crushing down on her tired mind. The feelings overwhelmed her, her eyes flooded with tears, and her exhausted body crumpled as Lili came barreling down the hill and tackled her with wide open arms.

"You did it, Carey!" Lili cried.

"I guess I did," Carey said breathlessly. "I thought I was dead for a minute," she added, shocked to still be alive.

"Good! Sister, you have done well. Let us go find the others." Alsoomse said, placing a tired hand on Carey's shoulder. Then she began to limp down the trail as Lili helped Carey up from the ground.

"You were supposed to stay hidden until I called," Carey reminded Lili as they walked through the brush.

"Oh, Carey, you guys killed them all!" Lili said, with triumph.

CHAPTER 18

The Battle Within

AREY AND LILI ENDURED THE WAITING. The *plan* had been simple. Once they got rid of the animals then they waited at the halfway point for Ella, but now it did not feel so simple. As the seconds ticked by Carey tried not to look at her watch again and again. Her mind was screaming. *Where are they? What's taking so long?* They felt like poor children that had endured winter but were not quite certain they would have a Christmas. As the moments dragged on, Lili became squirrelly with impatience, and Carey worried.

Alsoomse's leg was bleeding profusely. During their walk her temporary bandage had slipped. She would have to fix it before she lost too much blood. Limping about as they waited, she collected some moss, then she took out her knife and scraped the bark from a white willow tree. Returning her blade to its sheath, she popped the wood shaving into her mouth and began chewing. She rested beside the tree for a moment, before she shuffled over to a fallen log. She unbound the wound and sucked in her breath as she removed the red rag. The coyote's teeth had sunk deeply into her leg, but she was not too concerned. She had been wounded before. Leaning over she took two handkerchiefs that Carey offered her from her backpack, then used the moss like a bandage. She placed it firmly against her wound and tied it in place with the cloths.

When Alsoomse was finished, Carey stood up. She paced back and forth like a tiger in a cage. Lili began chewing on her fingernails. Her eyes glazed over with concern.

"Where's Ella?" Carey asked in a huff. "She should have been here already."

"Spring comes when it is ready, no matter how long you wait for it. Patience, sister," Alsoomse said. "Sit," she commanded, gesturing for Carey to join her on the log. Carey ignored her.

"Carey, I'm sure they're just delayed," Lili said, trying to help.

"Delayed? They're taking..." Carey cut off her reply. She thought she heard something. "What was that?" she stopped pacing and strained her ears to listen.

"I don't hear anything," Lili said, but then they all heard it. Through the woods they heard a voice calling. Their ears tingled with anticipation. They hoped it was Ella or Patty, but it was too far away to be sure.

They grabbed their spears and headed toward the sound. Despite the pain, Alsoomse set out at a trotting pace. Lili was trying her best, but her short legs could not keep up with the older girls, so they were forced to slow down. After moving at a frustratingly slow pace, they finally reached the hills near Aphina's camp, but then the noise had stopped. Carey was starting to wonder if her mind was playing tricks on her, when they heard it again. In mocking tones, they heard a voice pretending to be her sister's.

"Carey, help! Help me! I need your help, sister," the airy high-pitched voice was coming from over the hill and straight from Aphina's camp. Alsoomse and Carey froze when they heard it. Lili shuddered, and said, "Carey, that's not Ella." The little girl wilted, as if all the life had been siphoned out of her. She sat down hard on the trail. "She's—she's caught Ella." Two solitary teardrops trickled down her cheeks. The weight of her despair seemed to slow them down.

Carey's knuckles were white. As she gripped her spear, her fingers clenched so tightly that her joints popped. The anger she felt made her blood throb in her veins. Her ears drummed with every beat of her heart. *They were so close. How could this happen?* She tried to clear her head. She looked at Alsoomse for encouragement, but her face was void of expression. Lili reached up for Carey's hand and started scratching her thumbnail with her own fingernail. She knew what that meant. Lili was afraid. Some people twirled their hair around their fingers, others bit their fingernails, some chewed on their lips, but for some unknown reason, this habit had always been Lili's nervous little tick. She had done it ever since she was a toddler. Taking a deep breath, Carey muttered to herself, *I have to figure out something.* She was determined, but distracted. That mocking tone was infuriating. How was she supposed to plan or even think with those words running through her head?

After the third and final call for "help," Aphina stopped her play acting. They all heard her smooth confident voice calling over the hill, "Little ones, you might as well come out. We all know you have no options left. I have your sister and mother dearest. I would hate to see them get hurt."

Time stood still. Defeat stood triumphantly before Carey. Lili was talking to herself, mumbling something about thinking truth. *She is in no condition to go down there. If things are over, at least I can save my sister,* Carey thought.

"We can fight. It is not shameful for warrior to die in battle. My people consider it great honor," Alsoomse said, leaning on her spear. Carey saw the determined set of her jaw and the hard look in her eyes, and knew this was not empty boasting, but as she looked over her friend, she also noticed that her injured leg was bleeding again.

"We will go and fight if we need to, but not if it means losing my mother or sister," Carey said, deciding on a course of action and swallowing down the bile that rose in her throat.

Lili tried to get up and join them, pulling out her pocketknife with a shaking hand. Carey suddenly felt great pride swell in her chest as she looked at her littlest sister. She knew she was probably frightened out of her mind, but she was still determined to go with them and help if she could.

"No, Lili. You stay here," Carey commanded firmly. "Find a place to hide."

"No, Carey," Lili started to protest with quivering lips. Her voice was shaking, but her eyes were intense.

Carey put a hand softly over her sister's mouth and said, "I can't afford to lose you too." Carey paused as her stomach lurched. Her sister tried to pull her hand away, but she pressed it a little harder. "I don't know what will happen down there, and I want you safe. If you have to, you can watch, but stay here, please."

Lili listened and then quietly nodded her head. Carey kissed her sister's forehead and whispered, "I love you. Stay safe." Then she turned to Alsoomse. Aphina impatiently called again, "I am waiting," dragging out the last syllable for emphasis.

The two girls hefted their spears with weary hands and headed over the hill. The moment they were out of sight, Lili dropped to her hands and knees and crawled to a bunch of trees on her left. Beside these bushes sat their backpacks, the ones her sisters had left behind. She figured this would be a safe place to hide. She should be able to watch everything from here without being seen.

Aphina smiled devilishly as she saw the two young ladies walk over the hill. They were barely even women. The taller of the two was willowy with light skin and eyes and long blonde hair. She recognized instantly that the face was a younger version of mother dearest's. It was striking how similar their features were. As for the shorter one with darker skin and raven black hair, she looked quite beautiful. She was dressed

in leather deer skins. *Where did they find this one?* Aphina chuckled to herself in wonder. She also noticed that the shorter one was limping, and that her leg was bleeding.

The girls raised their spears in a threatening way when they reached the bottom of the hill. This was to be expected. The dark one was clearly practiced in the art of fighting, but Aphina had to give mother dearest's daughter some credit for her determination. She clearly had no idea what she was doing, but she would fight.

"Tut, tut, none of that now," Aphina said, standing beside Ella, who was tied up. Resistance was useless. She knew the game was over. She had captured their queen and had only to make a single move for checkmate.

She had time. They did not, so she waited. The girls seemed to be weighing their options as they walked forward, trying to put themselves in a better position to attack her. As she watched like a spider watches her web, she thought she saw what bordered on rage in the taller girl's eyes. The seconds ticked by, and Aphina decided they needed a little reminder of who they were dealing with. She pulled her curved knife from its sheath and poked it into her captive's side. Ella flinched and tried to pull away from the blade, but Aphina grabbed her hair with her free hand and yanked her back.

Both girls stopped in their tracks. "Stop!" the blonde one shouted. "What did I tell you? We all know you have no options. Throw the spears and knives away," Aphina said, poking the knife into her skin, causing Ella to gasp a little.

"Okay, okay, just don't hurt her," the tall one said, throwing down her spear. She looked over at her companion, who was clearly frustrated. After a commanding nod from mother dearest's daughter, the other spear was at last thrown down. "And the knife, wild one," Aphina added. With a disgusted click of her tongue, the girl removed her belt and knife and threw them to the ground, then stood with her arms crossed and her face stern.

"Now sister dear, take this rope and tie up your friend, and do it well," she said as she threw a rope to Carey. "Make *sure* it is good and tight. I would hate for someone to get hurt by accident," Aphina added the last words with an icy edge.

This can't be happening, Carey screamed to herself, but what could she do? All she knew was that twenty feet of old rope lay at her feet.

She moved as slowly as she possibly could to pick it up, anything to give her a little more time to think. Her numb mind tried to formulate some kind of plan, but they all fell apart each time she chanced a look at her tied-up sister. Ella was tense, trying her very best to keep the knife from pressing any farther into her side.

Alsoomse limped as she turned away from Carey. Without protest, she placed her hands together behind her back. Carey could not read those downcast eyes. At first her fingers forgot how to work, but after a few seconds a defiant desire fortified her resolve. A sudden determination to keep fighting started her fingers working. She hoped she could tie a loose knot but still make it look tight. Her heart drummed distractingly in her ears, the *thump-thump, thump-thump, thump-thumping* drowned out all other sounds. She wished she had paid more attention to her father's teaching. He had shown her how to make one or two trick knots, but she was not very good at them. She hoped this one would work. All she could do now was hope that the rope around Alsoomse's right wrist was loose enough.

"Now her legs, deary," Aphina commanded.

Carey bent down and tied up Alsoomse's legs. She was hoping the one loose hand would be overlooked if the rest were bound properly. Once she was done, Carey helped her friend sit down. Standing, she was about to turn when she heard Aphina call over her shoulder.

"Put your hands up in the air and back up to me. Carefully." The last word was added like a period at the end of a pointed sentence.

As Carey approached, Aphina bent to pick-up a second bundle of rope. The wretched lady shoved Ella to the ground, who landed on the grass with a grunt. Carey noticed that her sister was no longer threatened with a knife and a little glimmer of hope welled up in her. As Aphina sheathed her knife so that she might grasp the rope with both hands, Carey tried to drop her arms. But before Carey's arms had moved an inch, Aphina's strong hands locked around her wrists like handcuffs. It had happened in an instant, and before her mind could even register the pain, both her arms were wrenched behind her back and pulled up between her shoulder blades.

"Do not play with me, dearest. You are not a woman yet," Aphina hissed in her left ear. She gripped both her wrists with one hand and used her free hand to bind Carey's arms. Her shoulders were sore with the strain and ached horribly by the time Aphina plopped her on the ground.

At least Alsoomse's ropes are loose, Carey thought, but

as soon as she thought it, it seemed as if Aphina noticed the light in her eyes. She turned to inspect Alsoomse.

"Let us go and check on your warrior friend, shall we dearest? You never can trust anyone but yourself. That's my motto," Aphina said, as she tapped on the end of Carey's nose with her finger.

Carey felt like she was grasping at sheets of paper scattering in the wind. Her hopes, flittering right in front of her, were just out of reach. Maybe, just maybe she would not notice the rope. But when Aphina tested Alsoomse's bonds, she noticed the loose knots around one wrist, and Carey watched as the last fluttering sheet of hope was caught on a violent updraft and whirled off into the afternoon sky. Alsoomse tried to resist at first, but Aphina was too fast. The princess strained on the ropes and looped them around the young woman's wrist a few extra times, just for good measure. Then she tied them off in a complex knot. It was over. Carey and Alsoomse knew it. Alsoomse closed her eyes and began singing a dirge, in what Carey assumed was the Blackfoot language. The music did not help her mood. The minor tones of the melody were beautiful, but they gave the camp the eerie feeling of approaching death.

Carey scolded herself for being slow to react. She had had that *one* moment. If she had been a little quicker, she might have been able to overpower this slight woman. Her father had told her that she was always scrappy. This false guilt only lasted for a brief instant, because the next moment Aphina hefted her like a sack of potatoes. Without even a grunt she slung her through the air and up onto her shoulder. That is when she realized that she had never even had a chance to overpower this woman. Her face reddened as she was carried off to the other side of the camp and placed by her mother. She knew she was slight, but she would have never guessed that a woman as slender as Aphina could be that strong. Without a pause to catch her breath, Aphina walked over and quickly hefted Alsoomse and added her to the small group. After her final trip, at least Carey could console herself with the fact that they were all together. Ella was now lying next to her mother. Then Aphina checked her fingernails to make sure she had not soiled them and began to hum to herself. It sounded like a lullaby. She stood over them for a moment, her hands on her hips, one eyebrow cocked and a slight smirk on her face. Unconsciously, she stretched out her arm as if waiting for a bird to land on it, but before her hand reached to it full extent, it was drawn back and clenched into a fist. Carey heard the humming falter for a note or two, as the woman looked at the camping table. It was a minor disruption though, and the notes regained their normal meter as Aphina looked away from whatever it was on the table. Carey noticed that her captor's eyes gleamed dangerously and watched as she turned gracefully around and walked to the fire pit. With effort Carey pulled her eyes away from the tall woman and inspected the camping table. There she saw the lifeless remains of a crow. Jerking her eyes away from the mass of red and black feathers, Carey was startled by Aphina's next move. She was trying not to wonder why the woman had placed the blade of her long knife into the glowing embers of the campfire.

Aphina was satisfied now, though her pet had died. It should be confessed that she wanted to save him more than she would have admitted, but the bird's wounds were too extensive. She would have to comfort herself with the lie that she did not really care and would get another pet soon enough. She walked over to where the mother was sitting all tied up, nice and neat, like a present. *Finally, all the loose ends are taken care of,* she thought. But then something tickled at her mind. *What was it?* she wondered. Then it struck her. She had forgotten about the last little urchin. *What about the youngest? I wonder where*

she has run off to. Well, no matter. I am sure she is hiding in a hole someplace. Once I unlock this cursed book, I will deal with her and everyone else in this miserable, strange world. She steepled her fingers together and approached her prey.

"Mother dearest, it is time to talk. You see, I have your children, and now I will have the answers I am looking for," Aphina said in a calm voice that sounded worse to Patty than screaming.

Mackay was standing hidden in the doorway. All the smoke was gone. It had been gone for a quite a while. It had taken her forever to get the pages out of that deer skull, but she had finally managed it. She had been bright with excitement then, but her fairy fire burned a deep blue now as she watched the events unfolding outside.

What am I going to do? she thought. Yes, she had the papers, and she could pull them along if she tried, but *who* could she give them to? Aphina had everyone tied up.

The events had jarred her. Memories involuntarily flashed before her mind's eye: flames consuming fairy houses, the smell of smoke, gloved hands catching fleeing fairy folk, friends and family screaming in terror. Mackay was haunted by these old demons and was ready to give up as waves of old emotions overwhelmed her. The constant flashbacks distracted her thoughts, but then a light broke through the darkness. She realized that not everyone was captured. Lili was not tied up with the others at the camp. Hope flooded her heart and her fairy fire burned bright yellow for a brief moment.

As quickly as hope came, though, it was followed up by lifeless fact. She might have a chance of getting the pages to the group in the camp, but the hills were just too far away for her to reach. It would take her hours to drag these papers up there, especially if she did not want to be seen. Lili might be free, but there was no chance of getting them to her. Frustrated, she crinkled her nose and stuck out her tongue at Aphina as she watched her walk confidently before her prisoners. She was so smug it made Mackay angry. As she thought it over though, she knew that her friends did not have hours to waste while she dragged these pages up the hillside.

"Well, Mackay," she said, talking out loud to herself (which is a very normal thing for a fairy to do), "you might as well try to get the book to someone. You never know what might happen. If you stay in the cave you will just get caught by Aphina anyway, sooner or later. You might as well try." That last part, about being caught by Aphina, brought images of being put into a lantern again, and they were more than enough motivation to get her moving.

Before she left, she pulled a few loose threads from Aphina's sleeping mat and used the red strings to tie the pages into a tight roll. She thought she would look like a wood cutter hauling logs over her shoulder, but at least the load would be manageable. The next thing she must do was to extinguish her fairy fire. It took two or three tries, but she finally suppressed her feelings enough so that she did not burn. All those swirling bits of passion would have to be locked up safe and sound for now.

She looked around the corner one last time and quietly started her journey before she could second guess herself. The plan was to get the pages to Patty, even if she was tied up.

CHAPTER 19

Questions and Answers

PHINA WALKED MAJESTICALLY IN FRONT of mother dearest, drawing from all her countless hours of tutoring as a child. Her incessant instructors had drilled into her the use of body language as a symbol of dominance and control. She paused and pulled the knife from the coals and checked the blade. The last two inches were glowing bright orange and heat was shimmering off the forged steel tip. She watched from the corner of her eye as she inspected the blade longer than was necessary. She was waiting to see if she had everyone's full attention. Once she was sure she had it, she placed the knife back into the hot coals. She had learned from past experiences that it never hurt to add emphasis in such cases,

and to give enough time for her implications to sink in. All people had fears; even she had fears. At a time like this, the key was to use their fears against them. At least, that was how she saw it, my reader.

Aphina watched her prisoners like a curious boy inspecting a bug he has caught right before he squashes it. She thought that mother dearest was trying to hide her concerns, but she could see it in her eyes. Aphina was pretty certain that this woman would never talk under normal circumstances, even if she tortured her. She had that quiet determination and strength that would keep on resisting, even under the threat of great personal danger. *But every nut can be cracked*, Aphina thought. As she thought it over, she calculated that mother dearest's weakness was her daughters. She would talk, she was sure of it. Sooner or later her love for them would be her downfall. That was the way with love—it was weak. She *would* yield in time. She would yield for them.

The remembrance of love made Aphina shiver. Her dusty heart quivered, and painful longings coursed through her. Even locked far away in her prison house of regret, her heart had a way of reaching her. Her right eyelid twitched as scenes flashed before her eyes, and she felt anew those old pangs of grief. She must banish her old ghosts. She grappled for control as the memories of her little blonde-headed sister came haunting her once again. By sheer determination she shoved the thoughts away, fanning the emotional flames with her anger and bitterness. By the time she walked over to mother dearest, her face was a mask of calm once again.

"How does the book work?" Her voice was cool and calm, but as pointed as the tip of her knife.

Patty clenched her teeth. She knew she had very few options. At this point all she could hope to do was to delay this woman. She waited as long as she felt was safe before answering, "By reading it."

"Reading it?" Aphina enquired, seeking for the truth. Peering down her nose, she spat out, "I have read the whole cursed book, woman. I do not have time for your delays. I want straight answers." With these words she walked back over to the girls and looked at them with threatening eyes, purple flames burning within them. "No half-truths. No deception. Out with it! My patience is wearing thin, and believe me, mother dearest, you do not want to make me angry," Aphina said, patting Carey on the head as a reminder.

Aphina watched the internal conflict with feigned indifference and saw mother dearest make her decision. It was written clearly in her eyes. *Victory! The lock has sprung,* she thought eagerly.

"A person from outside the book must read it. When they do, the book works," Patty murmured through clenched teeth. She had confessed the truth of it, and it galled her to no end. She could see no way around telling this woman what she wanted to know.

"Ahhh, so that is how this curious little thing works. Interesting. Let us give it a try, shall we? But nothing too serious. I still do not trust you... completely."

Aphina glided over to her table and began to flip through the pages. She looked up from them though, for she felt a brooding stare. Looking over to her captives, she saw the hard, brown eyes of the woman glaring at her. *That one has lots of spirit,* she thought.

"Girl, what is your name?"

"Alsoomse," she answered defiantly.

"What an odd name. I have never heard its like before. Is it of the common language? I think they call it English here," Aphina asked, lost for a moment in sheer curiosity.

"No, it is Piegan Blackfoot. You would not know us, for our people do not allow workers of evil medicine to live," Alsoomse said, and spat on the ground beside her in contempt.

Aphina was impressed by her boldness, but the name had triggered something in her memory. *Blackfoot, Blackfoot... yes, what was it?* She knew such a name was not from her world, for she knew all the primitive peoples, and none had such an outlandish name as Blackfoot. Staring sightlessly at the book, something clicked into place and everything became clear. *The book. I read that name in the book.* Aphina's eyes snapped their focus back to the table and flipped through the pages once again. *Where was it? I know I saw it here somewhere,* she thought greedily.

There, there it was, on page three hundred and fifteen, 'Blackfoot.' It sat right in the middle of the second paragraph. Scanning the lines, she found Alsoomse's name. *So, she is also from the book. Well I think I can use this,* she thought confidently.

Aphina flipped to the last page of Alsoomse's story and then turned to Patty. "Mother dearest, you are not being totally honest with me. I think you are hiding something, and that is not good."

Patty looked confused. She was trying to figure out which part Aphina had discovered, and all the while Aphina waited. Her face was smug and arrogant, like a cat playing with a trapped mouse.

"How did Alsoomse get out of the book, mother dearest?" Aphina asked.

"I don't know. I wasn't there," she said truthfully.

"Yes, yes, I think you were visiting with me by then," Aphina said with a cool smile, "If you cannot tell me that, I think you can tell me something *else* I want to know. How do we send her back?"

Patty hesitated as long as she dared, but with a huff of frustration she finally answered, "A reader must finish Alsoomse's story. When she reads the last words, she will go back into the book."

"Hmmm, thank you, mother dearest. That was very enlightening," Aphina answered. She was temporarily satisfied and added a royal nod of her head in acknowledgement. Walking over to her table, she lifted the book and approached Carey. "Dear—Carey, is it not?" Carey gave a small nod, "Yes, well, be a good girl and read this page for me. *Now.*" Aphina's order laid emphasis on the last word. Certain of obedience, she held out the open book with her porcelain white hands, the beautiful pages inches from Carey's nose.

Carey looked at the book helplessly. She knew it was the last page of her friend's story. She stared through tendrils of Aphina's long white hair that hung irritatingly in front of her face and wished she could give them a good yank and kick the book away. Being helpless made her angry. Finally, Carey looked at her mother and received a quick slight nod. Though she did not want Alsoomse to leave, she would have to obey. The only thing comforting her was the fact that her friend would be free from Aphina once and for all when she was back in her own story.

"I'm sorry, Alsoomse. We'll miss you," Carey added before starting to read. Alsoomse nodded at her in her normal stoic way, then answered, "I am sorry too, but maybe someday Nahtoosi will allow us to meet again."

Tears rolled down Carey's cheeks as she finished the story. They watched as the young warrior faded away. The ropes that bound her fell limply to the ground as she disappeared. In the end the only thing left of her were shimmering Northern Lights that floated in a pulsing stream back into the book.

"Now we are getting somewhere," Aphina said with a laugh, which was much too melodious and refined to be described as a cackle. The large volume closed with a sudden snap, sending the scent of old vellum up Carey's nose. The evil young woman turned and placed the book safely back on the table.

Lili had been hiding in the bushes the whole time, and now she was scolding herself for being afraid. Everything felt like cold Jello inside and was flip-flopping around in a sickening way. She had watched with incredulity as Carey and Alsoomse surrendered. She had seen everything that was going on at the camp. She had even covered her eyes more than once, but then had watched through laced fingers.

Just when things looked to be their darkest, Lili almost swore that she saw something. "What is that?" she asked out loud. Near the trunk of her mother's tree was a blinking light. She was fairly certain Aphina could not see it from her angle but being up so high she could just see it over the little rise. It was right behind her mother. Every few seconds it was as if a tiny light would blink for an instant and then stop, as if its wire had shorted out. As she looked at the spot intently, she was quite sure of herself. It was not her imagination. It blinked blue, red, yellow, white. Each blink was followed by a long pause between each color. Sudden hope fluttered in her breast. *It must be Mackay. She must have rescued the stolen pages,* Lili thought, then falteringly she admitted, *but if no one gets the chance to read them, then Aphina won't go home.*

Lili knew that Mackay needed a distraction, one that would work just long enough for the fairy to get the pages to her mother. Her mother would also need time to read them. *But what can I do?* she thought. She was trying to think, but her fear, an unfortunate companion for the last few minutes, was whispering doubts into her ears. The accusing hiss of its voice kept telling her that the situation was hopeless, and she could do nothing. She was only a little girl after all. "All right. Breathe," she said to herself. "What did mom say? Think truth! Think truth, Lili..." she cut her words off as suddenly a light bulb flashed in her mind and she remembered something that she had forgotten. It was a long shot, but the only shot she had at this point. She began rummaging through the backpacks and found the dirty white tablecloth with chili stains all over it. *Thank you, Carey, for always packing too much,* Lili thought. Today of all days she was glad her sister never left anything behind. She hoped the red stains would look like blood. Quickly, before she could second guess her plan, she took off her clothes, wrapped it around her body like a dress and fastened her belt over top of it. She fussed with it and tried her best to get it to look just right. She needed it to if she was going to play her part. Then she crawled over to the ashes of the burning leaves and covered her face, arms, and legs in the pale, ghostly soot. She pulled off her bandana and rumpled her hair into a disheveled mess. She did not have a mirror to look at herself, but all her preparation would have to be enough.

With one last deep breath, she stood up. She brushed off a stray leaf from her ripped skirt with shaking hands and started down the hill toward Aphina's camp. With each step she mumbled the words, "Think truth." She hoped the words would calm her stomach. She needed something to keep her from paying attention to her churning desire to be sick. When she reached the grassy clearing at the bottom of the hill, she called out Aphina's name.

Aphina was humming again. She was taking some time to think through the implications of this new discovery, but then she heard a young voice calling her name. *That's strange. That voice almost sounded like...* She did not finish the thought. From the corner of her eye she saw a little girl walking toward her.

Carey's and Ella's jaws dropped. They blinked their eyes repeatedly as they saw their little sister walking into the camp wearing what look light a tattered, bloody, white dress. They started shaking their heads, exaggeratedly mouthing the words, "GO BACK," but trying not to make a sound. Their only hope was that Aphina had not noticed her.

Aphina could not believe her eyes. It was Lily, but how could she be here? Her mind darted between the little figure before her and old memories. She was rocked with the thought, but it had to be her. It was same slight figure, the same almost white-blonde hair. The figure moved with that same stiff and unsure posture, the same odd way her sister had been when she had to deal with complex court etiquette and had looked to her older sister for help. *No, it could not be, it must not be. It must be another vision, another memory. Another walking nightmare.*

As the specter took a step closer, a sudden picture of her little sister's wrecked body flashed before her vision. The blue eyes were open but lifeless. The little body was cold and limp. She could hear her own wails once more. She felt the anguished cries of pain welling up within her all over again. She could feel once more the soft hand as she clutched it, trying to hold on, trying to bring her sister back. The memories jumbled now; the sobs of her pain mixed with the startled sounds of the hunting party. She could hear them. She did hear them. They were shouting to each other, "The king and princess are dead!" It rang in her ears once more, like the baleful clanking of a mourning bell ringing in her ears. Tears clouded her eyes as the little figure took another step forward. Then it called out coolly, "Aphina."

Aphina's whole body shook in tremors. *How could it be?* "Is that you, Lily?" Aphina cried.

"Yes, I am Lili," the soft voice answered.

"But how can it be? You are dead," Aphina wailed. Her knees were beginning to buckle, but she forced herself to take a stumbling step forward. It had been so long, but the wounds in her bleeding heart were as raw as the day she had received them. All her well-trained composure and control was lost. The years of dammed-up emotions burst and her eyes flooded with unrestrained tears. Her grief was too real to be contained any longer.

"Aphina, you have left me no choice, so I have come to you," the wispy voice called as Lili took another step forward.

"Lily, I am sorry. I did not mean for you and Father to die. Why did you have to go? Why did you leave me? You were my heart, and—and love flew away from me that day. It died in me when I watched you both go! My little bird! My little bird," Aphina cried out these last words. Her chest heaved, her legs wobbled, and she struggled to stand. Great sobs erupted from her throat, crowding out her words. "P-Please forgive me. Do not leave me again..."

She pleaded as the little figure continued to creep forward step by determined step. Aphina fell to her knees, her unrestrained grief was finally too much for her. Her thin ivory hands gripped each other as if in penitent prayer. Her chest heaved and she gasped for breath between wails, as she gazed upon the torn white dress covered in red stains. Her white willowy fingers reached out hopefully as a little arm reached out to her. Her bloodshot eyes longingly looked through her tears to the outstretched little hand and traced the slim arm up to a serious, concerned face, but as she fixed her gaze on it, she instinctively knew something was wrong. Suddenly her mind cleared. The shock of understanding blew away the fog that her emotions had caused. *Those eyes are brown! My Lily's eyes were blue*, came the realization.

"You are not my Lily!" Aphina declared, jumping up in rage. "What is this?" she choked out as she swiped the tears from her eyes.

Aphina realized that the masquerading little wretch was no longer looking her in the eyes but was glancing over her shoulder. Curiosity being what it is, she was forced to look behind her. Turning, she saw what had caught the impudent little girl's attention. In the midst of the prisoners, mother dearest was kneeling. Her head and shoulders were held up high in the hopeful air of deliverance. One hand was still tied, but she was free in spite of it. Triumph had resurrected and defeat had died, for in her free hand, mother dearest held pieces of parchment. She was holding them in a shaft of light shining from an opening in the canopy above. A little impish fairy hovered over mother dearest's shoulder. The thing burned brilliantly. The glowing bright yellow fire caused spots to dance before her eyes.

When she grasped what had happened, how she had been fooled, a guttural growl rumbled from Aphina's throat and burst into a scream. She turned with heaving chest, her anger mounting, and stared at the wicked child.

The little girl did not flinch, though Aphina intended to wither her with one look. With a fire in her own little brown eyes she said, "You're right. I'm not your Lili; I'm hers. And it's time for you to say goodbye."

Her murderous rage boiled over, and Aphina grasped for

her belt knife, but as she clutched at thin air, she realized too late that the blade was still stuck in the fire. Then she felt it, the pull of magic. Like the tugging of mighty ropes tied about her whole body it was dragging her to the book. In one last attempt at revenge, she struck at the little girl's face, but all that touched the soft cheek was wind and vapor. Before she could land the blow, her hand had dissolved into inky mist. The transformation rippled up her hand into her arm. The dark fog that rolled over her skin enveloped her, and they watched as she turned into nothing but a dark cloud. The very air sucked at Lili's stray hairs and pulled them towards the book, as Aphina fought to remain in their world. Then Lili heard the flapping of wings and cawing of crows, echoing through the trees. The misty wailing form condensed into a ribbon of pure essence. In the blink of an eye, the midnight black stream of smoke sped to the book and disappeared into its pages, and an invisible hand closed the book's leather cover with a resounding thump.

The last echoes of Aphina's cries faded and left a profound silence in their wake, which was shattered a moment later by relieved cries of joy.

When it was all over, Lili almost collapsed, but she willed herself to stand.

"Lili!" Patty cried. Their elation destroyed all that remained of their composure. Lili's first clumsy steps stumbled into a sprint, as the sound of her mother calling her name reached her ears. Relief delighted her, just like it does when you see your mother after a long bout of homesickness at camp. Lili crashed into her mother, the pair squeezing each other in a monstrous hug, smothering each other in kisses, and wetting each other with tears of joy. Impatiently Carey and Ella scooted themselves over, and Lili sat there hugging them all in a long, ardent embrace. Peals of laughter broke out, and everyone smiled. Lili took Ella's pocketknife and cut their bonds. Once everyone was free there was another round of hugs. Then, as the rapture slowly subsided, they basked in the realization that it was over. They could go home.

Carey was the one that broke the silence when she finally asked her sister, "Lili, how did you know that would work?"

"I didn't," she admitted.

"Then why'd you do it?" asked Ella, amazed at her sister's pluck.

"Because I remembered something. Back at the house we read that Aphina's sister's name was Lily, and that she had blonde hair like me, and we are about the same age. Then I remembered her picture in the book even looked a lot like me. So, I figured if I dressed up and acted the part, her imagination might make up for the rest. Plus, Mom always says, when you're afraid, think truth. I just figured that Aphina might be so mean all the time, because she was running from her pain and hiding from the truth. If she had to see Lily, that might be enough to beat her."

It was quite a simple thought, they realized, but it had worked. After all, my reader, it does not have to be a big idea to be powerful—it just has to be a true one.

"I love you Lili-lou," Patty said as she gave her daughter another huge hug.

"Where's Mackay?" questioned Ella.

Lili stopped hugging her mother for a moment and looked around. Everyone's joy changed to concern. Four pairs of eyes scouted around for any sign of the little fairy, but her fire was nowhere to be seen.

"She was here a minute ago, while I was reading the end of the story," Patty said. "She was right above my shoulder."

"Let's go look around. You never know with Mackay. She's probably putting together a victory bouquet or something," Ella suggested.

They looked high and low, all over the place, under every object in camp and around every tree. They talked it over and decided she might be playing a fairy game of hide and seek, so they walked all over calling out, "Mackay, come out, come out wherever you are! We're not playing games anymore!" But in the end, they could not find her. Everyone was standing around scratching their heads when Carey walked over to the camp table for one last look. "I know where Mackay is," she called.

They all perked up, "Where?"

"In the book," Carey said. The book was open to the picture of the fairy-seller. "See?"

As they hunched over the page, they saw it. All the lanterns were aglow, just as they had been before they had read Mackay out of her story. "We forgot that she was from the same story as Aphina. When Aphina went back in, she went back in too," Carey said sadly.

The air was thick with silence, and everyone had lumps in their throats. Ella swallowed two or three times, then whispered, "I sure will miss her."

"Me too," added Lili.

"Well, I'll tell you one person I won't miss," Patty said, and they all finished the thought together, "Aphina!"

CHAPTER 20

Home

T HAD BEEN THREE GLORIOUSLY NORMAL days since their adventure had ended, and everyone's cuts and bruises were healing quite nicely. There had been moments during the first day that the cawing of a lone crow in the garden, or the creaking of a floorboard in the house had brought sudden apprehension, but each time it left just as quickly as it had come. The third morning began with the smell of bacon and pancakes and the possibility of being totally normal. Everyone agreed it was just how they liked it to be. They had had more than enough adventure for one summer.

On the third afternoon the girls were enjoying a lazy ride on the green swing which hung on the little white house's porch.

Carey was sitting in the middle and Ella and Lili had their heads lying on both of her shoulders. Their legs were slowly pumping back and forth rocking the swing ever so gently. They were doing nothing, really, but doing nothing can be fulfilling and necessary after a difficult time. Each girl gave a contented sigh. It was nice to be able to just sit. To listen to the birds. To smell the scent of the mint and basil growing in bunches near the porch. To be normal and calm.

After lifting her head from Carey's shoulder Ella asked a question in a drawn-out, lazy kind of way, "Carey, you think Dad will make us get rid of the book when he gets back home tomorrow?"

"I don't know," she answered.

"I sure hope not," she said, rousing a little from her lethargic mood. "I mean, I don't want any bad guys getting out, but I really want some way to remember Mackay." With these words Ella crossed her arms in frustration. "We didn't even get to say goodbye," she protested. Carey knew that disappointment always made her sister annoyed.

"Yeah! I wish we could've gotten to say goodbye," Lili added sympathetically, in full agreement with her frustrated sister.

A gray cloud seemed to dim the sunny afternoon sky as the girls sighed and went back to swinging. The next moment, a ball of pulsing, giggling, yellow fire shot in front of their faces and they heard a tiny voice say, "Why all the gloomy faces? Aren't you happy to see me?"

"Mackay!" the girls shouted and showered the little fairy with so much affection that she beamed a lovely shade of pink. They screamed, giggled, and hugged *each other* (one does have to be careful of hugging a fairy too hard after all). Interrupting each other, they all tried to get the next word in. At last Ella shushed everyone and told Mackay that she could begin by telling them all about what had happened since her return to the book. They would then tell her how their adventure had ended. Everyone's minds were so perfectly absorbed in the telling and hearing their tales that it took about twenty minutes before anyone even realized that Patty was leaning in the doorway with the screen door propped open. She had been watching the whole time, standing there, polishing an apple on her kitchen apron, wearing a contended, happy smile. When they finally noticed her, they all stopped talking.

"Thanks, Mom," all the girls said together.

"No problem. I figured you all had some unfinished business," Patty admitted, taking a bite out of the apple.

As they told their stories again, the sisters fit in all the details they had left out the first time, and Patty leaned there, quietly listening. She slowly ate her apple as she looked out over the garden. After she had finished the very last bit, having taken the time to go around the scrawny core twice, she knew it was time for Mackay to go home. Gently she hinted, "Girls, it's probably time to say goodbye."

"Yes, I must go. Now that Aphina has been defeated, we fairies have lots of work to do to rebuild our homes in the forest. But don't worry, I am quite sure I will remember you, as much as you remember me," Mackay said. She kissed each girl on the tip of her nose. "I wish you all could join me there."

"Well, we can *in a way*," Carey realized, "when we read your book."

As she followed Patty back through the screen door, Mackay waved an enthusiastic goodbye, which caused her curls to bob back and forth. She seemed happy, but they noticed that once she passed through the door her fairy fire began to flicker between a tentative brown and a melancholy blue.

One by one all the girls got up and went into the house, following their mother and Mackay into the family room. On the dining room table next to an empty teapot and cups, lay the book. It had been removed from its spot—a new glass display case that hugged one of the bright yellow walls of the living room. Patty had decided to buy the display case just to have a safe place to keep the book locked up. (Secretly the girls hoped that meant that Mom wanted to keep the book too, despite the danger). The glass door was standing open with the golden key still in the lock. Patty cleared her throat, picked up the book, and turned to the last page of Mackay's story.

Each girl stood around Patty, forming a little circle around their tiny fairy friend. They watched as Mackay danced along the book's edge and Patty started to read the last words of her story. They wanted the words to be read slowly so that they might savor each one. They wished their mother could read them over and over again—for the feeling they had was just like the one we all get when we finish a great book. They wished it did not have to end, but like all good stories, adding extra chapters would only cheapen it. The time had come to say goodbye.

Mackay kept waving and smiling with mischief, sparkling as she slowly disappeared and her fairy fire faded from sight. Patty closed the book and placed a hand on the cover and stroked it gently. Carey and Lili gave their mom a quick kiss on the cheek and then walked back onto the porch. Ella, on the other hand, hung around as Patty put the book back in its case. She watched as her mother turned the key in the lock. It made a little metallic click as she did. Then she removed the key and put it back in its hiding place.

Patty lovingly placed her arm around Ella's shoulder as they turned and headed outside. "Mom, do you think we'll ever see her again?" Ella asked.

"I don't know, kiddo. Only time will tell," Patty answered, giving her daughter a smile and a kiss as she opened the screen door for her. "How about we go outside and live our own story?"

ABOUT THE AUTHOR

John A. Sommer was born in the state of Indiana, but quickly moved to Northern Michigan. There he spent a large portion of his childhood at a 120-acre Christian camp. In these wide spaces he spent his summer days, wandering the woods, swimming in the lake, catching frogs and snakes for fun, shooting at the archery range and pretending to be Robin Hood, riding dune carts as much as he was allowed, and playing with the new friends he made weekly.

As he grew his parents moved again and shortly thereafter he started his first "real" job as a strawberry picker. Since his first job (which only lasted one summer), he has held jobs in many other lines of work: being a grocery clerk, a sawmill worker, a landscaper, a waiter, and a cook in an industrial kitchen.

One year after college he and his wife, who was expecting their first child, moved halfway around the world to be missionaries in Ghana, West Africa. This has been his life's calling ever since.

During his time in the tropical sun he has discovered and re-discovered many things. Guitar playing, reading great books, and learning how not to sweat in the 100+ degree weather are just a few of them, but one of greatest treasures he shares with his beautiful wife and four girls is the joy of telling a story.

ABOUT THE ILLUSTRATOR

John D. Neiner has been drawing ever since he learned that a pencil wasn't for chewing. After realizing that his dream to be a pirate on the high seas was an occupation most likely fraught with hazard, John decided to pursue his aspiration to become an artist. He began his intensive art training by copying all the pictures from his Little Golden Books. Over time John began to have his own ideas and found that creating designs from his imagination brought him the greatest thrill.

Born into a ministry home with a father who is a pastor, John has enjoyed the unique perspective of life from within a fish bowl. Little did John realize this arrangement afforded him the greatest opportunity to develop the observation skills he would need in the future.

Endlessly fascinated and inspired by the mighty works of God in creation, John is an avid mineral and fossil collector. Thanks to the good nature of his wife Erin, John's mineral collection is on permanent display in their living room.

No stranger to wearing a lot of hats, John is also an assistant pastor of a small Baptist church in New England, alongside his father the senior pastor. John and Erin spend their time cultivating with their three boys their own fish-bowl experience in the beautiful hills of New England.

A NOTE ON THE TYPE

This book is set in *Aluminia*, a text-optimized revival of the typeface *Electra*, commissioned by Leterform Archive and digitally restored by master letterer and type designer Jim Parkinson. The original *Electra* typeface was designed by typographer extraordinaire W. A. Dwiggins in 1935 for use on the popular Linotype machines. Working from authentic Linotype drawings, Jim Parkinson brought this classic face into the digital realm while maintaning the energy, legibility, and unique letterforms of the metal original.

The drop caps appearing at the start of each chapter were drawn by John D. Neiner specifically for this project and are titled *Cadmus Cap* after the character Zao Cadmus described in this book.

Typeset by Neiner Creative
Pittsfield, Massachusetts
Printing and binding by Versa Press
East Peoria, Illinois

Designed by John D. Neiner